**At the end of the day, we can endure much more
than we think we can.**

Freda Kahlo

Cast of Characters

who live in Orchard Lane

MARYANNE at number 1
Divorced middle-aged ex-nurse. Recently moved to Melbourne from a semi-rural town.

MILDRED at number 2
Elderly widow.

VIVIENNE at number 3
Young woman recently separated from her husband.

MANDY at number 4
Young mother, married with three children.

JOANNE at number 5
Nurse who works in a busy hospital. Lives with brother.

MRS FOSTER at number 6
Widowed older woman who fosters children. Joe is living with her now.

JACKIE at number 7
Married middle-aged woman who breeds poodles.

MARIA at number 8
Middle-aged woman married to Anesti.

ELOISE at number 9
Young woman who teaches yoga.

LISA at number 10
Young mother of two little girls married to Sam.

STAVROS and THEODORA Cafe owners on High Street.

Contents

Introduction

Maryanne is a kind, friendly, middle-aged woman who likes people and makes friends easily. Because of this, too often she finds herself involved in other people's worries and problems. Having suffered and survived her own traumas in the past she has become an understanding, empathetic listener and supporter to others. In the past the burden of other people's troubles eventually became too heavy and took its toll on her wellbeing. It is for this reason she first began to consider moving from her semi-rural acreage to a small property in inner Melbourne. Hoping to make a fresh start and avoid involvement in other folks' concerns, she made the move.

In her new home in Orchard Lane she meets a diverse group of people all from different walks of life. As she becomes close to some of the women, she once again finds herself embroiled in a variety of trials and tribulations of her new friends.

Orchard Lane is a small street which runs from High Street into a park which was once an apple orchard. Little cottages, numbering ten in all, are evenly placed opposite each other down both sides of the narrow street. A large part of the orchard was rezoned and houses were built in the years after World War Two. Older-style houses and being close to the city makes it an attractive place for young families to live.

ORCHARD LANE
HIGH STREET
BUS STOP
CAFE
Maryanne 1
2 Mildred
Vivienne 3
4 Mandy
Joanne 5
6 Mrs. Foster
Jackie 7
8 Maria
Eloise 9
10 Lisa
ORCHARD LANE
APPLE LANE
PARK

1

Maryanne

When Maryanne heard the postman blow his whistle at her front gate she realised she had been painting for about four hours. Putting the paint brush into a jar of water, she walked to the kitchen, filled the kettle, pressed the button to begin the boil then strolled to the front gate. There were several letters in the letter box, mostly bills but one was addressed to her in familiar handwriting.

The letter was from Steven, her only son — only child actually — who had been living and working in the UK for several years. He usually sent her an email once a month and occasionally made a phone call but a hand-written letter was most unusual. She made herself a pot of tea and a sandwich and sat down to read the letter.

When she finished reading she was a bit annoyed and also perplexed. Why hadn't he written of his new plans months ago? Why had he waited for her to move to her new house to ask her such a thing? The letter said that he was planning to return to Australia with his English wife, Hilary, and they were negotiating two places for them to work in a medical centre in the semi-rural township of Kelvington. Both were doctors and had been working as general practitioners in England. Steven's wife was expecting their second child and he was asking Maryanne to move to Kelvington to be near them and to help out with child minding.

If he had asked a few months ago she would have agreed without hesitation, but as she had just moved into her new home, she did not want to move again so soon. For goodness sake, she said to herself, it's so expensive to move and there's a lot of planning and hard work involved in the process. She did not want to disappoint him but she thought he was asking a bit too much.

Maryanne had been living not far from Kelvington and had made the big move back to the city. The house she had moved into was in a quiet street of ten little cottages. They all looked much the same from the street, but Maryanne's was a beauty. It had belonged to a young couple who had renovated and extended the house, turning it into a modern, open-plan dwelling. Small, but perfect for a couple or a single woman such as herself, but not for the young couple with a surprise package of triplets. She had only been living in the house for a month when she received Steven's letter.

After finishing her tea and sandwich she returned to painting the living room walls and became so caught up in the task that the next thing she was aware of was the light fading and birds singing their end of day chorus. After showering and getting ready for bed, she sat back and admired her newly decorated room.

"I love this little house and I'm going to enjoy living here," she said out loud.

She did not think about the letter again that day.

2

Orchard Lane Residents

Once Maryanne had completed all the painting and had put all her belongings into place, she felt that she was ready to begin her new life in the new neighbourhood. Her plan was to see who her neighbours were by spending some time working in the front garden. It was a neat and tidy garden but she had decided to change it completely and had settled on a French-style parterre garden, estimating that it would take her two or three weeks — enough time to see who was living in each of the other houses as she worked.

Maryanne's house at 1 Orchard Lane was the first house in the short dead-end street, which ran from a fairly busy High Street into a small park at the other end. Around the corner to the right on High Street was a small strip shopping centre and to the left a bus stop where buses ran half-hourly into the city. All very convenient, and she thought she could probably manage without her car most of the time.

After a trip to the local garden centre she was ready to begin her garden makeover. She pulled out and dug out most of the things she did not want and soon realised that was all she could manage in one day. She hoped that putting some of the unwanted plants out on the footpath would be a good way to see who her neighbours were if they came to help themselves. Filling several buckets with water she placed the plants into them and put up a sign saying, FREE TO a GOOD HOME.

Directly across the street at number 2 was a house just like hers except the front door needed a fresh coat of paint, the garden needed attention and the letter box was hanging at an angle on one screw. She noticed an elderly woman watching her from the front window but did not wave to her as she probably thought Maryanne could not see her and she did not want to embarrass the woman. About twenty past three, the smart-looking front door of number 4 next door to the elderly woman opened and out came a young woman carrying a small baby. They got into a car which was parked in the street and drove away. School pickup, Maryanne assumed, and yes, half an hour later the young woman returned with two young girls wearing school uniforms.

About 5pm a young person walked down from High Street and entered number 6. A 'person', thought Maryanne, because she was not sure of the sex of the figure. It sometimes happens that you will see a young man or woman who could be of either sex and this was one of those times. She was just about to go inside when a car pulled up at number 8 and out stepped a well-dressed young woman who rushed up to the front door and rang the bell. Almost immediately an older woman came to the door and handed over a baby to the woman, who turned, waved, and quickly put the baby in the car and drove away.

Quite a busy street, Maryanne thought as she poured herself a glass of wine to drink while she cooked an omelette and put a salad together. When eating her dinner she reflected on what she had seen today and how different it was going to be living so close to all these different people who she hoped to get to know. Well, they seemed different to her, as she had been living on a large property with no near neighbours and most of the people who had lived around her were middle-aged like her. She imagined it would be nice to have young mothers and little children in her life again.

The next day she began work early on the garden, digging over the soil and putting down string to separate the garden and grass area from the new path she was planning. She placed pots of lavender along the fence where she was going to plant them to make a hedge and positioned pots of roses in their allocated spots. Feeling tired, she had stopped to admire the design when the door of her immediate neighbour at number 3 opened and a heavily pregnant blonde woman emerged and wobbled to the gate.

"Hi," she said, peering over the fence. "That's going to look very nice."

"Thank you," Maryanne said. "Yes I think it will look good when I finish. I'm your new neighbour — Maryanne."

"Nice to meet you, I'm Vivienne and as you can see I am very soon to be a mother. Actually I will be very glad when this pregnancy is over and done with; it seems to just go on and on, and I am so uncomfortable."

"Yes I remember it was not much fun, but when you get the baby you will be so happy. It's worth the wait, you'll see. When is the baby due?"

"Next week, thank goodness," Vivienne replied.

"Let me know if you need any help at all," Maryanne offered.

"I wouldn't mind some company — would you like to have a cup of tea with me when you knock off?" Vivienne asked.

"Okay, I'd like that. I'll come in about four, is that alright?"

"Yes, I'll see you then."

3

Vivienne

At four o'clock Maryanne went next door to Vivienne's for a well-deserved cup of tea. Walking down the hallway the aroma of freshly baked scones made Maryanne's tummy rumble.

Vivienne looked at Maryanne, who had changed into clean shorts, and thought to herself how good she looked for a woman of middle age. Her legs were long and tanned and her body was trim and healthy looking. Out loud she said, "I will be glad if my body ever returns to normal."

"It will in time, you will be so busy with your baby," Maryanne answered reassuringly.

"I am so glad to have a nice new neighbour next door. When Tony and Marina told me they were moving I was devastated and I miss them so much," Vivienne said, looking quite sad. "We had become very good friends but when their triplets were born they realised they had grown out of their lovely home."

Vivienne poured the tea into two pretty cups and handed Maryanne a plate of homemade scones. "Please eat some, I made them this afternoon."

"I can smell them. I'm ravenous; I'll probably eat a few, thanks," Maryanne said, taking a scone and heaping it with strawberry jam and cream.

"Mmm, delicious. Did you make the jam?"

"I did. I like home-made jam and it's so easy when you have the time."

The two women sat and chatted for hours and found they had quite a bit in common in spite of the age difference. They both loved cooking, movies, reading and making patchwork quilts. Maryanne was very surprised to hear that Vivienne was a single mother-to-be.

"I am still married but I'll be divorced soon, my husband doesn't want any children and it was a bitter pill for him to swallow when I became pregnant and I insisted I would keep the baby," she said. "We argued and he walked out; for all I know he could have already shacked up with another woman by now."

"That's very hard on you and sounds very final," Maryanne sympathised.

"Yes, it's not the best situation to be in, that's for sure."

"Do you have family to help you?" asked Maryanne.

"My parents and sister live in Sydney but as my father is very ill Mum can't leave him. He has Parkinson's disease and had a stroke a few months ago and I haven't told them that Phillip has left me. I don't want to burden them anymore. They have enough to worry about."

"Do you have friends who can help you?"

"I have a few girlfriends but they are all working full time or busy with children of their own."

"Well, I am offering my help; so we can exchange phone numbers today and you can ring me any time. That's if you want to," Maryanne quickly finished.

"Thank you Maryanne, that is very kind of you—I might need some company sometimes. I don't know much about babies, only what I've been reading in self-help books."

After Maryanne went home Vivienne had a shower and got ready for an early night. As she sat up in bed trying not to feel sorry for herself, she realised that Maryanne moving in next door could be a gift from the goddess of motherhood. Picking up the book she had been reading recently she attempted to read but it just did not hold her interest. Running her hand over her belly she said, "Goodnight little baby, it won't be long now, we will be meeting soon." Then she turned off the light, falling asleep almost at once.

About 2am Vivienne awoke as a sharp pain and a strange tugging feeling rippled through her abdomen. At the same time she was aware of liquid seeping from her body and then another pain hit her.

"Oh my goodness, I'm going to have the baby tonight, I had better get up and ring a taxi," she muttered to herself.

Her attempts to get out of bed were hindered by more contractions, which were a lot more intense than she had ever imagined. She had always planned to call a taxi and get to hospital on her own. She had envisioned this happening slowly, and hopefully during the day, but it was not to be. Vivienne quickly realised she was in trouble and needed help. Fortunately, she had put Maryanne's phone number straight into her mobile phone which she now picked up to call her.

"The baby is coming and I can't get out of bed to open the door, I can't walk and I think it's too late to ring a taxi—I don't know what to do!" she yelled to Maryanne.

"It's okay, are there any windows open?" she asked.

"Yes the laundry window's open but you will have to climb the fence."

"That's okay, I'll be there in a minute."

Grabbing a chair from the deck, Maryanne put it against the side fence and climbed over into Vivienne's back garden. When she entered the bedroom she found Vivienne crying and moaning and rocking from side to side.

"I didn't think it would happen so quickly," Vivienne wailed. "And I didn't think it would hurt this much!"

"It sometimes happens very quickly and with very little warning. How far apart are the pains?" Maryanne asked.

"They just seem to be coming one after the other."

"You could be in transition and about to go into the second stage. Let me have a look."

Maryanne confidently removed Vivienne's pyjama pants which were saturated with amniotic fluid and gently parted her legs.

"Oh yes, the baby is almost here," she said. "Stay as you are and pant when the pain comes back. I will get some towels."

Maryanne quickly returned with clean towels and a wet face washer which she wiped over Vivienne's hot and bothered face. "Are you comfortable on your back or do you want to lie on your side?"

"I don't know," she cried.

"Did you ring an ambulance?"

"No I haven't had time to ring anyone but you. I'd always intended to use a taxi to get to hospital."

"Okay, don't worry, I've done this before. Just try to breathe through your nose and out through your mouth until the contraction is over."

"But I feel like I want to push," Vivienne managed to say.

Maryanne had a quick look and said, "Oh my goodness, this is all happening very quickly—I think you are ready to have your baby. When you have the next contraction, put your chin on your chest and push."

Vivienne began to push and the baby's head began to emerge but the umbilical cord was around its neck.

"Don't push with the next contraction, just pant," Maryanne instructed as she gently slipped her fingers under the cord and eased it over the baby's head. Then, "You can push now."

Vivienne pushed a few more times and the baby was born.

"It's a girl," said Maryanne as she lifted a black-haired, olive-skinned baby onto Vivienne's chest. The baby cried, Vivienne cried, and so did Maryanne as she covered the baby with a clean towel.

The baby settled on Vivienne and began rooting around seeking a nipple.

"Oh she wants to feed," said Vivienne, assisting her baby to find her nipple.

"Good, let her, the sooner the better. I'll ring an ambulance now and when they come they can cut the cord with sterile scissors."

Vivienne kept her baby on her bare chest and allowed her to suck. Every few minutes she kissed the top of the baby's head and murmured soft loving words to her.

Maryanne stayed and cleaned up after the ambulance had taken Vivienne to the hospital. She changed the bed and did a load of washing, hung it on a clothes horse, then went home to bed.

Within an hour of giving birth Vivienne was settled into a bed in the maternity ward with her baby by her side. Gazing at the newborn baby girl with the rosebud lips and the long dark eyelashes she was filled with overwhelming love and wonder that she had produced such a beautiful little being. She could not help thinking about how Maryanne had come to her rescue in such an unexpected way. Who would have guessed that an experienced midwife would move in next door just at the time she, Vivienne, needed her.

"Maryanne was so calm when you were rushing out to meet me," she murmured to the child. "I think we are very lucky to have her next door."

As she drifted off to sleep thinking over the birth, she could not help wishing that her husband Phillip had been with her.

4

Joanne

Vivienne rang Maryanne when she arrived home with the baby three days later. "Do you want to come in to see the baby?" she asked.

"Yes I want to see you both," said Maryanne. She had been expecting Vivienne to call her when she arrived home and had made a cake and a large pot of vegetable soup for her. The baby was asleep and Vivienne was sitting reading her mail when Maryanne entered.

"What can I do for you?" she asked.

"Sit and talk to me, I wanted to talk to you about the birth and how calm and efficient you were. You really came to my rescue. Thank you so much!"

"Oh well, I am a nurse and midwife but I haven't delivered a baby for a while, however your delivery was very straightforward so it was quite easy. It was faster than most though."

"Well I can't thank you enough, I am extremely lucky to have you as my neighbour and friend, and because you helped me I have named the baby after you. She is Maryanne, but I might call her Annie or Mary."

"That's so nice and a very big compliment, thank you Vivienne."

The front doorbell rang. "I'll get it?" checked Maryanne as she moved towards the hallway.

Vivienne looked up and smiled as Maryanne returned accompanied by a good-looking dark-haired woman of about thirty who was carrying a large bunch of flowers and a wrapped gift. Maryanne went to the kitchen to make a pot of tea and returned and sat with the two women.

Joanne, who lived next door at number 5, was a nurse who shared the house with her partner Anthony, her brother John and his girlfriend Emily. She and her brother were originally from the Barossa Valley in South Australia, where their parents owned a small vineyard. The brother and sister had come to Melbourne to work several years ago and bought the house in which they now lived with their current partners.

After relating the story of the birth of the baby and cooing over her beauty, the three women settled down to enjoy another cup of tea and a slice of the home-made cake Maryanne had baked. Between them, Vivienne and Joanne told Maryanne about the other residents they knew in the street. Mrs Kerr who lived at number 2 was a widow. She had a daughter and an intellectually disabled son who visited about once a week. Next to her at number 4 was a young couple with three children. At number 6 was Mrs Foster who had fostered many children.

"I have seen Mrs Foster and also a teenager going into her place. Is that her son or daughter?" Maryanne asked. "I was not sure which; it was hard to tell from a distance."

"Well, we don't know either and we don't like to ask. I suspect he is a boy because of the clothes he wears but his face is soft and his hair is long and curly," said Vivienne.

"I think she is a girl and just a bit of a tomboy fighting her femininity," said Joanne.

"What about the people in number 8?"

"They are a middle-aged Greek couple with several grown-up children. Mrs Papas looks after her son's baby when the daughter-in-law is working."

"How do you know everyone so well?" asked Maryanne.

"We have a Christmas street party every year and often meet in the park at the end of the street where we walk our dogs," Joanne replied. "Plus this being such a short dead-end street it's easy to work out who is who."

"Sometimes we will have a picnic and everyone just joins in," Vivienne added. "It's a very friendly place to live; we are all friends but not in each other's houses all the time."

Maryanne stood, preparing to leave. "I had better get going. I'm off to the hardware shop to choose some paint for my front door."

"What colour?" chorused the other two.

"Something bright; now that I don't have to please anyone other than myself I'm going for an unusual front door colour. Maybe crimson or purple, I'm not sure yet."

"Is it okay if I take a few of the plants you put on the footpath?" asked Joanne.

"Take as many as you like," Maryanne replied. "I'm glad they are going to be rehomed."

After the front door closed Joanne looked at Vivienne and said, "Maryanne is full of surprises. Is there anything she can't do?"

"My thoughts exactly," Vivienne replied.

5

Maryanne decided on a semi-gloss aubergine-coloured paint for her front door and a dark green trim for the door frame and front windows. She spent the day preparing the timber and then gave everything a coat of paint. On the first day she saw Mrs Kerr's daughter and intellectually disabled son arrive and attempted to make eye contact with them as they left. They did not see her, or pretended not to. As the day went on she noticed Mrs Kerr watching her from the window and she raised her hand and waved to the elderly woman, who waved back.

Mrs Kerr rested her arthritic hands on the window sill as she peered through the glass and observed with interest her new neighbour, who seemed to be working extremely hard at totally changing the appearance of the house. She was not sure that she liked what was being done; she was used to the house looking as it had for years and now it had a strange coloured front door and a completely new garden style.

The next day when Maryanne saw Mrs Kerr at the window she stopped painting and walked across the road. She made a gesture as if drinking a cup of tea, hoping the woman would respond and she did. Mrs Kerr opened the door and they introduced themselves.

"Would you like to come over for a cup of tea, Mrs Kerr?" asked Maryanne.

"That would be very nice dear, thank you," she replied. "Are you throwing out those plants on the footpath?"

"Yes, take whatever you want," Maryanne said. Looking at Mrs Kerr's arthritic hands, she asked, "Do you need help to plant them?"

"I should be able to manage one or two," the elderly neighbour replied.

They settled in the living room, which looked out onto a pretty garden at the back of Maryanne's house. Mrs Kerr said she had not been in the house since an older couple who had lived there moved out five years ago when and Tony and Marina moved in. She had been very friendly with the older couple, Mr and Mrs Jones, who had been her age, and their children had all grown up together. She told Maryanne that her husband had died ten years ago and she was lonely but at the same time happy to be on her own most of her time.

"I walk to the library once a week and sometimes catch the bus to the city but not often," she said. My daughter visits about once a week but I wish she wouldn't come. I don't like it when she comes."

"Well," said Maryanne, looking at this sad woman who had all the tell-tale signs of a difficult life: her clothes were way out of fashion, her hair was badly cut and she just had a worn-out appearance, "How about you come over to my place for morning tea a couple of times a week? I'm always up for chat."

"That would be very nice, how kind of you," she replied.

Sensing that the elderly woman was lonesome Maryanne said, "I still have a few things to buy for the garden, would you like to come to the garden centre next time I go?"

"Yes, I would love to. It's not easy for me to get there and I'd like to plant some seedlings in the front garden."

"Okay, next time I'm going I will let you know. Can I call you by your given name?" asked Maryanne.

"Yes, it's Mildred," she replied with a smile. And as she crossed the road she thought to herself, "What a nice woman. I hope we can be friends; it would be nice to have a new friend so close by."

Maryanne watched the thin woman return to her home and noticed she had a bit more pep in her step as she walked across the street. It occurred to Maryanne that Mildred had been an attractive woman once but wearing an old navy blue cardigan over a shabby grey dress with socks and slippers did nothing for her appearance.

6

Mandy

Maryanne finished the painting and continued to work on her garden, where she planted a few more flowers and shrubs to complement the new colour scheme on the front of the house. As she had been hoping to meet more of her neighbours, she was pleased when Mandy, who lived next door to Mildred, popped over to look at the discarded plants. They got talking and she told Maryanne she was sleep-deprived due to her young baby who was difficult to settle day and night.

"To make things worse," said Mandy, "my husband Mark is always away because of his job. I feel like I am a single mother," she complained.

"I have plenty of spare time," said Maryanne. "Could I be of any use to you?"

"I couldn't impose on you," Mandy answered, feeling embarrassed that she had opened up so much to this new neighbour.

"I wouldn't offer if I didn't want to help."

"Really, are you sure?"

"Yes," replied Maryanne firmly. "Would you like me to come over before school pickup, or after, when you are preparing dinner, and I can take the baby for a walk in the pram?"

"Oh, that would be wonderful but how can I repay you?"

"You don't need to," said Maryanne. "I'll stay while you bath the children and get them to bed. I can't do it every night but maybe two or three times a week. I can come over tonight and see how we go."

Mandy returned home wondering what she had just done. Should I invite a virtual stranger into my home to help me with the children? she asked herself. Yes. It will help me so much; I will give it a go.

An hour later, Mrs Foster at number 6 crossed the street to look at the plants, which were beginning to wilt. She complimented Maryanne on the newly painted front door and her new garden. She hung over the gate for a long chat and told Maryanne all about how much she liked children and how many children she had fostered.

"Did you decide to become a foster parent because of your name?" asked Maryanne, grinning.

"Everyone asks me that. No, I just like children, and there are so many who are in need of some TLC."

"Is the teenager living with you your child or a foster child?" asked Maryanne.

"No that's Joe. Joe has been with me on and off for several years. Comes and goes, comes and goes. Very troubled is Joe," replied Mrs Foster sadly.

"Well I hope I get to meet Joe one day."

"Joe is a bit of a loner, no friends, won't see the parents, doesn't talk much, it's very sad."

"Next time I see Joe I'll say hello," Maryanne said.

"That's good of you, but don't expect much response."

They parted promising to get together for a cup of coffee and a chat soon.

Later that afternoon Maryanne crossed the road to help Mandy and they agreed that she would take the baby for a walk in the pram. Mandy finished feeding the baby and handed her to Maryanne who put her on her shoulder to bring up wind. Once the baby had burped, Maryanne wrapped her up, popped her into her pram and headed out the front door. Standing at the front gate she wondered which way to go, to High Street or to the park. She decided on the park, walking the short distance to the end of the street into the quiet green space. The park had once been part of an apple orchard which had been sold and subdivided to build houses a long time ago. There was a path around the perimeter that had been worn by walkers and cyclists and it was on this slightly bumpy trail that Maryanne began to walk. She was halfway around and the baby was sleeping soundly when she noticed a man lying under an old apple tree. He was accompanied by a dog, a Queensland Heeler, also asleep. As she passed neither of them stirred but on the second time around both the man and his dog opened their eyes and looked at her.

"Good afternoon," said Maryanne.

No reply from the man, who appeared to be rather surprised. On the third round the dog lifted its head and the man nodded to her. A fine-looking woman, he thought to himself.

Maryanne decided that when she returned the sleeping baby to Mandy she would offer to help for another half hour. The other two children were finishing their dinner so Maryanne ran the bath for them, tidied the kitchen and encouraged Mandy to sit and eat her dinner while the baby was asleep. When she left, the two older girls were playing in the bath, the baby was still sleeping and Mandy was very grateful.

After the success of that first evening Maryanne continued to take the baby for a walk two or three times a week to put her to sleep, and to help out with the other two children.

Running parallel with Orchard Lane was another street called Apple Lane which also ran from High Street into the park, so Maryanne was able to vary her walk. Sometimes she went through the park and other times she walked up to High Street, past the small strip shopping area and back via Apple Lane and the park into Orchard Lane. On one occasion, returning to Orchard Lane via High Street, she was upset to see Joe from across the road bailed up by a small group of teenage boys. Joe was obviously distressed, being pushed up against a shop window and surrounded by the boys who appeared to be enjoying the harassment. Maryanne hated any type of intimidation and particularly where it concerned one person being bullied by several others.

"Out of the way, lady with a pram coming through!" she said loudly, pushing the pram between Joe and the boys causing them to back off and run away, allowing Joe to escape.

Quietly she said to Joe, "I'm Maryanne, your new neighbour. Would you like to walk home with me?" Joe didn't answer but began to walk with her anyway.

"Do those boys always bother you Joe?"

"Sometimes, but I try to avoid them."

"Why are they annoying you?"

"They say I'm weird."

"You don't seem weird to me."

"I'm not weird, I'm just a bit different."

By this time they had reached the gate to Mandy's house.

"I'm going in here," said Maryanne. "Joe, if you ever want to talk to me about anything at all I can keep a secret. I won't tell anyone anything you tell me."

"Yeah," Joe muttered.

"I hope we can be friends Joe."

There was no answer. Joe walked quickly next door and entered.

Maryanne thought back to her act in pushing the pram between Joe and the bullies. I suppose that was a bit risky, she thought. It just shows what cowards they are.

7

Vivienne's Husband

Vivienne rang Maryanne one morning and invited her to come in for a chat that afternoon. Later that day the two women sat together in the living room sharing a pot of tea.

"My husband Phillip has finally been in touch with me and wants to visit to see the baby," said Vivienne.

"That's good, isn't it?" Maryanne replied.

"Well, yes and no. I don't know what's behind his sudden interest in the baby; it's probably just curiosity but maybe he wants to make amends, perhaps he wants to see his daughter and take responsibility for her."

"How would you feel about getting back together?"

"I'm not sure… I'll have to wait until I hear what he has to say. He really hurt me when he left."

"Well then, you just have to wait until he comes and take it from there. I'm sure he will make it obvious what the visit is about. When is he coming?"

"Tonight, and I'm nervous. I don't want to see him on my own but he won't be upfront with me if there is anyone else here. I'll fill you in tomorrow," added Vivienne.

Maryanne went home and began preparing a casserole which would provide several meals for her dinner over the next few days. At nine that night as she was preparing for an early night she received a phone call from a very distressed Vivienne.

"Oh Maryanne it was awful, he is really angry with me and refuses to believe the baby is his."

Vivienne was in tears.

"Do you want me to come in?"

"Would you please—if you don't mind? I need to talk."

Maryanne quickly went next door to be greeted at the front door by a red-eyed Vivienne carrying the crying baby.

"Come in, come in, Maryanne." They sat in the living room and Vivienne attempted to put the baby to the breast but she was so upset it took ages for her to settle down. Finally she relaxed and began to suck and before long had a full tummy and fell asleep, making it possible for Vivienne to speak.

"It was awful," she said.

"What happened, Vivienne?"

"Everything was fine until the baby woke up. I went to get her and as soon as he saw her he began to yell and rant about the baby not being his."

"Why would he say that?"

"Because he is a fair-skinned, red-headed man and the baby is olive skinned, which neither of us are."

"That can happen if there have been olive-skinned people in the family," said Maryanne. "She could be what is commonly called a throwback."

"Yes I told him that, because that is what I thought had happened. I haven't been with any other man since long before we were married. I am so upset by his accusation I don't know what to say or what to think. He just refuses to believe me and says the baby is not his and he wants nothing to do with me or her."

Vivienne was finding it hard not to cry again and the tears began to roll down her cheeks.

Maryanne moved to sit beside her, and putting her arm around her she said, "You can easily settle this by him having a DNA test you know."

"I know, we could settle it that way, but he would have to agree and I'm not sure that he would."

"Well, considering what he is accusing you of, he will most likely be more than willing, don't you think? It would make it easier to prove what he is suggesting, after all."

"I suppose so. I'll suggest it to him and see what he says. I'll have to tread carefully though, he is very angry."

Vivienne dried her eyes, stood up and carried the sleeping baby out of the room. When she returned she gave Maryanne a hug and thanked her.

"Let me know what happens and if I can be of any help to you," said Maryanne as she moved towards the door.

It was true that Phillip had ranted and raved when he first saw the baby. He could see she was a very beautiful baby but no way was she his child. Where could that dark hair and olive skin have come from? There was no one in his family who looked like that as far as he knew. He was sure the same could be said for Vivienne's family, and that made him very disappointed and angry. He had been feeling guilty about the way he had reacted to the pregnancy and was considering apologising to Vivienne, hoping she would forgive him so they could get back together again. Now he was adamant that would never happen.

8

Maryanne enjoyed the evenings she helped Mandy. Firstly she was doing a good deed, secondly she was making friends with her neighbours and thirdly she was getting exercise. As she headed towards the park one evening she encountered Mrs Papas standing at her front door holding a chubby smiling baby.

"Hello," said Maryanne.

"Hello," replied Mrs Papas, whose attractive face lit up when she smiled.

Before they could say another word a car pulled up and out stepped the young woman Maryanne had seen on several other occasions. She hurried through the gate, grabbed the baby, kissed the older woman and after strapping the baby into a car seat, she drove off.

"That's my daughter-in-law," said Mrs Papas.

"She's in a hurry," said Maryanne.

"Yes, she has to hurry off before my husband comes home."

"Have you had a bit of family trouble?" asked Maryanne.

"You could say that I suppose, it's ridiculous really and I'm in the middle of it."

Maryanne stood at the gate not knowing whether to ask why or just keep quiet. Mrs Papas seemed keen to continue the conversation and said, "It's all because of a Greek tradition. My son refuses to name his son after my husband—which is the custom—because he doesn't want his son to have a difficult name and he says there are already enough boys in the family with his father's name anyway. We do have two more sons who have named their boys Anesti after my husband but he thinks they should *all* have his name."

"Oh, I see," said Maryanne.

"My husband Anesti will have nothing to do with Ari until he changes his mind. They are both stubborn and neither of them will back down."

"Did your son get teased at school because of his name?"

"Not very much as far as I can remember, we called him Ari. There was one time when some children found out that his name was Aristotle and he was teased until the teacher told the children who the original Aristotle was."

"So does your husband know you are looking after the baby?"

"No, and if he finds out he will be very angry with me."

"What if he comes home early, what will you do?"

"I suppose we will have a big argument."

"Oh dear, that's difficult."

"Anyway I suppose something will happen to make both of them see sense."

Changing the subject she added, "I have seen you a few times since you moved in and noticed you gardening and painting; the house looks very nice."

"Thank you. My name is Maryanne, what is your name?"

"I am Maria," she said, extending her hand to Maryanne. "I hope we can be friends."

"We will, I'm sure. I had better get moving," Maryanne said and continued down the street to the park. She did two rounds of the park then walked to Apple Lane and up to High Street. The window of the first shop, a florist, was full of attractive pots containing large indoor plants. The second shop was a mixed business and the third and last shop was a cafe. Looking inside she noticed that it was very spacious and the seating, which looked comfortable, was arranged in hospitable groups. There was a display of delicious cakes and savouries under glass and two women were behind the counter chatting. Maryanne decided to go in and have a cup of tea and peruse the array of delicacies on display.

Seated at a table near the window she pushed the pram backwards and forwards hoping to keep the baby asleep. One of the women brought her tea and said, "Is that your grandchild you are looking after?"

"No, she belongs to my neighbour Mandy, I'm just helping her by doing a bit of babysitting."

"I thought I recognised the pram, it's quite distinctive. Mandy comes in sometimes with her mothers' group."

"You don't mind groups in during the day?"

"No. We have two book clubs as well as several mothers' groups. They all drink coffee or tea and eat something light so we are happy to have them."

"Well I might see you with a little group soon," Maryanne replied.

"We provide a bottomless cup of coffee," the woman added.

Walking home, Maryanne decided to act on her idea but thought it better to begin at her own home, so after dinner she drafted a short letter.

> *Dear Neighbour*
>
> *I have decided to begin a regular informal get together for the women of Orchard Lane. I have been involved in something similar in the past and found it fun and of great benefit to all. Next Wednesday at 10.30 you are invited to my home for morning tea. No need to reply, just come if you like.*
>
> *Maryanne @ number 1*

Before the sun went down she posted one in each of the letter boxes in the street.

9

Morning Tea

The following Wednesday Maryanne opened her front door at 10.25 in readiness for her guests to arrive at 10.30.

"Good morning," she said to Maria, who was the first to arrive.

"Hello Maryanne. I don't have the baby today so I was happy to receive your invitation."

"Come in, but don't worry, you can bring the baby if you want."

Maryanne glanced over the road to Mildred's house hoping to see her coming across the road and noticed a car belonging to Mildred's daughter parked in the driveway. Damn, she thought to herself, that means Mildred won't be coming, and to Maria she said, "I was hoping Mildred from over the road would be here but it looks like her daughter is visiting her."

As Maryanne showed Maria into the living room Maria commented, "They usually seem to visit her first thing in the morning."

"Yes I've noticed that, and after they leave she always seems upset," Maryanne replied.

Soon the living room was filled with friendly conversation and laughter. Maryanne made tea and coffee and handed round buttered fruit scones and tomato sandwiches. Mandy sat on the couch with her baby asleep in her arms and Vivienne settled on the other end of the couch breastfeeding baby Maryanne.

"Now that my baby has arrived we will have a lot more to talk about," Vivienne said to Mandy. "You can probably give me some advice as you have had three babies."

"I hear you have named the baby Maryanne?" said Mandy, smiling at Vivienne. "That's a coincidence—now we have two Maryannes in the street."

Vivienne began to laugh. "No, not really a coincidence, it's because Maryanne came to my rescue and delivered my baby for me. It's the least I could do to thank her."

"Really? I didn't know that; how wonderful," said Mrs Foster, who had just entered the room and seated herself between the two young mothers. The other women all listened with interest about the day Maryanne and Vivienne met in their front gardens and later that night Maryanne assisted in the speedy arrival of the baby. The doorbell rang, interrupting Maryanne's telling of the events. "I'll be back," she said over her shoulder as she headed to the front door.

Almost at once, following Maryanne back into the living room was a stunningly beautiful woman whose arrival caused the room to fall silent.

Looking around at the women seated in the room and without being prompted, the new arrival said, "Hello, my name is Eloise. I've just moved into the end house, number 9, and I am really pleased to be invited here because I don't know anyone in the area."

"You are very welcome," said Maryanne. "I haven't been here long myself which is partly why I decided to invite our neighbours to morning tea."

The women were introduced to Eloise and the chatter resumed. "I've owned the house for a while but I have just moved in," she told Maryanne. "I'm going to renovate the house and garden and make it my own little haven—keeping one room to use for teaching yoga," she added with a smile. "I want to change the garden a bit so I need to buy some plants and various other things from a local supplier. Is there somewhere nearby?"

"Yes, in the next suburb. Let me know when you are ready to go and I'll come with you if you like," Maryanne said. "I promised the woman across the road I would take her so maybe the three of us can go together."

By 12.30 the visitors had all departed and Maryanne tidied the room and cleared the dishes. Gazing out of the window, her hands immersed in a sink full of hot soapy water, she was astonished to see a healthy young fox emerge from beneath a bush against the back fence. The fox sat on the grass and groomed itself and as it turned around she was given a full view of its beautiful bushy tail. At first she thought she was seeing things but as it climbed onto a garden seat and lithely hopped over the fence she had to admit it was real. What a beautiful animal, she thought to herself. I suppose it must live in the park.

That evening she crossed the street to Mandy's house and took the baby for a walk in the pram. Passing the house where Eloise lived she wondered who lived next door to her at number 7. Stopping for a few seconds to admire the garden she noticed two black miniature poodles jumping at the wire door followed by a woman carrying two dog leashes. The dogs continued to jump excitedly until the woman commanded them to sit, which they did, and she was able to attach their leashes.

"Are you going for your usual walk around the park?" the woman asked.

"Yes, how did you know?"

"I have noticed you going past several times over the last few weeks. Are you Maryanne?"

"Yes I am. Did you get a letter from me?"

"Yes I did but I was unable to come, but I would like to if you are getting together again."

"Yes—next Wednesday, please come. Are you about to walk in the park?" Maryanne inquired.

"Yes. I'll walk with you if you don't mind. I'm Jackie and these dogs are Betty and Boo."

The old man and his dog were dozing as usual under the same tree. Catching sight of the two well-groomed poodles the dog stood up and wagged his tail. His eyes never left them as they walked twice around the park. As they walked, Jackie told Maryanne that since her children had grown up and left home she had been breeding poodles. The older dog, Betty, which had recently been neutered, was the mother of Boo, who was still too young to have a litter.

"Oh I would love a poodle. When will you allow her to breed?" Maryanne asked.

"In a few months' time she should be ready," Jackie replied.

The two women parted outside Jackie's house and she promised to be at the next morning tea.

Now I have met all of the women who live in the street except one, Maryanne said to herself as she looked at number 10.

10

Mildred had wanted to go to Maryanne's for morning tea but was prevented from doing so because of a visit from her daughter and son. They had their own keys and could let themselves in whenever they liked. She never knew when they would arrive and she just had to put up with it. She had never told anyone at all about her family situation and as soon as her daughter left each time, she tried to put the visit and all it involved out of her mind.

She liked Maryanne and valued the friendship which seemed to be growing, but being an elderly woman with low self-esteem and very little self-confidence, she left most of the invitations to Maryanne. She had not had a friend since the people who had lived in Maryanne's house had moved five years ago. Her only outings were to the local shops or library and as she did not drive she often felt sad and lonely. She wished Maryanne would knock on her door and ask her over again but she was uncertain about crossing the road to knock on Maryanne's door herself. Perhaps if she went into her front garden more often she would see her outside. Then she remembered that Maryanne took the baby next door for a walk in the evening two or three times a week.

Mildred saw Maryanne crossing the road carrying something across her arm. She went outside hoping to intercept her before she entered Mandy's house and greeted her. "Hello Maryanne."

"Hello Mildred, how are you?"

"I'm well," she answered.

"I'm just about to go for a walk with Mandy's baby but I have something to give you if you would like them."

She handed Mildred two soft cotton frocks. One was a striped blue and white shirt dress and the other a floral Liberty-print shift.

"I can't wear these any more and they are too good to throw out," she said. "I always try to recycle if I can."

"They look lovely," said Mildred, "thank you. Can I walk with you?"

"Yes please do, I would love the company," answered Maryanne.

The two women entered the park and began the usual circuit, passing the old man and his dog who both appeared to be sound asleep. The old fruit trees had small green apples beginning to develop and it looked as though there would be an abundance of free apples in a few months.

"What happens to the apples when they have ripened?" asked Maryanne.

"Everyone picks them but a lot just fall to the ground and are wasted," Mildred replied.

As they walked around the park for the second time, Mildred glanced over to the man, who was now sitting up, and gasped. "Oh my goodness!"

"What is it?" asked Maryanne.

"That man, I think I know him."

"Do you want to stop and speak to him?"

"No, just keep walking please," said Mildred, obviously upset.

Arriving at Mandy's front gate, Maryanne said, "I'll just take the baby inside; I won't be long, and we can go to my place for a chat."

Seated at the kitchen table a few minutes later, Maryanne asked Mildred, "What was it about the man in the park that upset you so much?"

Mildred sighed and took a deep breath. "He reminded me of my dead husband who I hated, and just for a moment I thought he had come back. I know it isn't him, he was much older than me and that man is more my age. I just got a fright, that's all," Mildred replied. "I feel a bit silly now."

Wanting to change the subject Maryanne went to the fridge and took out a bottle of wine, pouring two glasses. She sat down again. "I have a secret," she said. "I've seen a fox in my back garden. It's beautiful, its tail is so big and fluffy and it's well fed and healthy looking."

"I didn't know there were foxes in the city," said Mildred.

"Apparently there are more foxes in the city than the countryside. I'm going to keep quiet about it because some people hate them. So it's a secret, okay?"

"Yes of course, I'll keep your secret. My father and my husband would have killed it, they were both cruel men."

"Hmm," said Maryanne.

Changing the subject, she asked if Mildred would like to go to the garden centre on Friday, and Mildred readily agreed.

"A woman called Eloise who has just moved into number 9 wants to go to the garden centre so perhaps we could all go together," Maryanne said.

"I'll drive and we will leave at 9am so that we can start planting in the afternoon," she said to Mildred as she farewelled her at the front gate.

Mildred went home and tried on the two dresses, which were nicer than anything she had worn for years. Going to bed that night she felt a lot happier.

11

Unspeakable

Eloise knocked at Maryanne's front door just before nine on Friday morning and when she opened the door Maryanne was annoyed to see that the car belonging to Mildred's daughter was parked in Mildred's driveway.

"Damn," she said. "That means Mildred won't be able to come with us. Her daughter just drops in whenever she feels like it and poor Mildred never knows when she will turn up, plus she always seems upset after she leaves."

"I'll go and knock," said Eloise. "Maybe if we tell her daughter we have made plans she will still be able to come with us."

She walked across the road and knocked several times but no one answered the door. Maryanne joined her and they walked around the side of the house to Mildred's bedroom window. It was difficult to see inside but there was a lamp alight on a table on the far side of the bed. With difficulty Maryanne peered through the wire fly screen and a lace curtain and gasped. She was shocked and wondered if she was really seeing what she thought she was seeing.

"My god, I must be seeing things but I'm going to make sure."

She yanked at the side gate but it was locked so she ran out the front gate and next door to Mandy's place, where her side gate was open. Maryanne rushed through and climbed over the fence into Mildred's back yard. Banging hard on the back door it flew open, allowing her to hurry inside where she encountered Mildred's daughter standing at the kitchen sink, a tea towel in her hand, drying a teacup.

"What are you doing barging in here?" she asked indignantly.

"Your mother was supposed to go out with me this morning, where is she?" demanded Maryanne.

"She's still in bed," the daughter replied.

Maryanne headed for the hallway determined to find Mildred, and was met by Mildred's intellectually disabled son who was walking towards her doing up the zip of his jeans.

"What is going on here?" roared Maryanne. "What was he doing in Mildred's bed?"

"Mind your own business," said the daughter.

"This has just become my business!" Maryanne shouted at the top of her voice.

The daughter grabbed her brother by the arm and ushered him out the front door. "Come on, we are going," she said.

They left quickly through the front door, allowing a stunned Eloise to enter.

"What happened?" she asked.

Maryanne was visibly upset as she uttered, "He was having sex with his mother."

Eloise gaped. "Raping her, you mean?"

"Yes," said Maryanne, pushing open the door to Mildred's bedroom.

"Mildred," she said gently, "It's me, Maryanne."

Mildred was in bed with the blankets pulled up over her head.

"Oh Mildred, what have they been doing to you?"

Mildred did not answer but she was crying softly. Maryanne went to the bed and sitting down, she gently removed the blanket from Mildred's face and attempted to take her hand, saying, "You poor darling."

Mildred rolled onto her front, sobbing uncontrollably, her shoulders heaving. Eloise stood close rubbing her back in an attempt to comfort her. Eventually Mildred became quiet and lay still.

"Come on Mildred, let's help you up."

Mildred allowed herself to be eased into a sitting position. Eloise picked up a dressing gown and the women helped Mildred into it. Taking the older woman to the kitchen, Eloise made a cup of tea and some toast while Maryanne sat talking quietly with her. Mildred gulped the tea and nibbled at the toast then looked at the two women, who were studying her with sympathy and concern etched on their faces.

"No one has ever cared," she said sadly.

While Mildred was having a shower Eloise and Maryanne discussed what they should do to help Mildred.

"We should ring the police," said Eloise.

"I agree, but before we do anything we had better see what Mildred has to say."

Mildred told them she did not want the police involved. "This is the way my family is," she said. "It's been happening to me all my life."

"But it's a crime and he is your son."

"My father and then my husband always said it was the responsibility of the women in a family to help the men in that way."

"Well they were wrong, very wrong."

The three women spent quite a long time talking but Mildred would not change her mind about the police.

"Okay," said Maryanne. "But we have to get the locks changed on the front and back doors and have locks put on all of your windows."

"Yes, that would be good," agreed Mildred, brightening a little.

As Maryanne looked up a phone number for a locksmith and rang to make arrangements for the locks to be changed the next morning, she couldn't help thinking why Mildred had not changed the locks herself ages ago.

"You will be staying at my place tonight," instructed Maryanne.

Eloise went home and Maryanne helped Mildred to pack an overnight bag. They crossed the road and Maryanne put on the television for Mildred and made her comfortable on the couch. Later in the afternoon Maryanne went to the adjoining kitchen and began preparing an evening meal for the two of them. As she worked she wondered not only why on earth Mildred had not changed the locks but why she had not notified the police or her doctor, or done something to help herself. I suppose if it's been happening to her all her life she has just accepted it, she thought to herself.

Movement outside in the garden made her look up just in time to see the fox slink into the bushes carrying something that looked like a dead rat in its mouth.

12

Gardening

On the following Monday morning, Maryanne, Mildred and Eloise spent several hours at the nearby garden centre selecting a few plants for themselves and a dozen Australian native plants for Eloise. Eloise wandered off and was gone for a while so Mildred and Maryanne sat in the cafe and ordered coffee and cake. Mildred was wearing the striped dress Maryanne had given her which fitted and suited her slim figure.

"The dress looks really nice on you, Mildred."

"Thank you. I should refresh my wardrobe. I haven't bought anything new for years, I don't know why. You have given me a jolt."

Eventually when Eloise joined them her cheeks were flushed and she was grinning from ear to ear.

"What are you looking so happy about?" asked Maryanne.

"Well—I have just been chatting to the owner of this business and I think I'll be coming back, he is divine."

"How nice, you never know where you will meet someone you like, do you?" Maryanne replied.

Eloise did not answer, she just smiled.

That afternoon Maryanne helped Mildred to plant her seedlings then they crossed the road to put Maryanne's new shrubs in her back garden. Mildred went into the kitchen to make a cup of tea leaving Maryanne to start the digging. Prior to pushing the spade into the soil, she heard a soft animal sound over by the back fence. Before she could investigate Mildred called her to come and have a cup of tea. Deciding not to mention the fox again, Maryanne sat with Mildred and they simply enjoyed the peace and quiet of the garden. When it was time to go Maryanne emphasised to Mildred that she could ring her at any time if she felt the need. As it was time to take Mandy's baby for a walk, she escorted Mildred back home where she gave Maryanne a new key to her front door.

Meanwhile Eloise was at home spending time in the garden daydreaming about the man she had met that afternoon at the garden centre.

13

Vivienne

Vivienne's baby was thriving and had become a calm, easy infant who smiled and gurgled happily whenever she saw her mother's adoring face. Vivienne was amazed at how the maternal instinct had kicked in and taken over her behaviour and attitude to almost everything she did. She was still breastfeeding and usually slept with the baby beside her at night. She had been told she should not sleep with the baby but she was very careful to keep her in her arm and away from pillows. Really, she wanted the baby near her at all times.

She had shortened the baby's name to Mary and sang all the songs she knew about Mary. 'Mary had a little lamb', 'Mary Mary quite contrary' and 'Mary Mary' an old pop song. The baby was entranced by her mother's voice and stared at her as she sang even though Vivienne was no singer.

Her husband Phillip had been to see her again and reluctantly agreed to a DNA test which he said he knew would be negative. He was so sure the baby was not his. Vivienne was adamant that the baby definitely was his, so they both agreed it was the only way to settle the matter.

14

One night when Mildred got out of bed to go to the toilet she fell, hitting her head and breaking her arm. She lay on the floor in a daze for several hours then when she was able, she struggled to her feet and put herself back to bed. In the morning her head ached and her arm throbbed every time she moved it. Knowing she was in trouble she rang Maryanne who rushed over and found Mildred in a terrible state. She made her a cup of tea and gave her some painkillers then said, "I could take you to the doctor but you have hit your head and you are going to need that arm X-rayed and plastered, so I think we had better go to hospital."

Following a long morning at the hospital, Maryanne took Mildred home to her house knowing that she would need help for at least a week or two. Mildred was very grateful and told Maryanne that in all her life no one had ever looked after her.

"What—not even your mother?"

"No, not even my mother, not that I can remember anyway."

Once again Mildred was made very comfortable at Maryanne's place and they spent a lot of time talking. Mildred began to tell Maryanne about her childhood and her disastrous marriage. Her father had been a violent, nasty man who terrorised his wife and children. When Mildred was six, her mother took her youngest child and vanished, leaving Mildred and her eight-year-old brother to fend for themselves with their father. It was at that young age that Mildred's father began sexually abusing both her and her brother. He boasted that he was a religious man but he was cruel and vicious and the children were too scared to tell anyone about their home life. People felt sorry for her father because his wife had left him, and he pretended to be a good man who had been deserted for no good reason. He sometimes hinted to people that his wife had run away with another man. Mildred didn't think this was true because she did remember her mother being fearful of her husband.

Maryanne listened to the awful story of Mildred's tragic life and could not help feeling how fortunate she had been to have both wonderful parents and a loving husband. She found it difficult to sleep after some of the things Mildred told her and she knew that the story was not over because of the awful situation with Mildred's son and daughter.

During the time Mildred stayed with Maryanne, she told her about her brother Norman who had run away from home at sixteen and she had not seen him since. Norman had begun to stand up to his father and they had had many arguments and even physical fights. It was after one of these fights, during which Norman had hit his father, that he had gone. The time between Norman leaving and her father dying had been dreadful for Mildred but fortunately for her, two years later, when Mildred was sixteen, her father died suddenly.

"I found him sitting up in his lounge chair, his face was as blue as the shirt he was wearing that day. I got a fright but quickly realised that I was free at last so I was happy. I didn't care that he was dead."

She added, "I was glad and thought my life could be normal at last."

Regrettably there was no money left to her and the house, which was rented, was priced beyond her means. The shop she worked in paid her only a meagre wage and her future looked bleak.

At the church they had attended there was an older man who took an interest in Mildred and he persuaded her to marry him before she was eighteen. This decision was one she quickly regretted as he became as abusive and domineering as her own father had been.

Mildred had two children, one who died in an accident and the daughter who visited her. "I thought it was your son who visits you with your daughter?" Maryanne said.

"No, he is her son and my husband is the father," Mildred answered.

"Oh my goodness, what a terrible life you have had. It's hard to believe," exclaimed Maryanne.

"Well it's all true and there are other awful things which I try to forget about."

"So your daughter was abused by her father just like you were."

"That's why my daughter brings my grandson to me; she thinks I should suffer like she did. I think she hates me because I didn't protect her from him but I couldn't."

"Oh, Mildred."

"As I said to you the other day, you are the only person who has ever helped me."

It was stressful for Mildred to disclose the reality of her life and after revealing her story she became quiet and withdrawn. Maryanne left her alone for an hour then presented her with a glass of wine and something to eat which helped to cheer her up.

After two weeks Mildred went home and was supported by council workers who visited her several times a week to assist her with showering and housework. She would have liked to stay with Maryanne but was aware that she could easily outstay her welcome and that was the last thing she wanted.

15

Wednesday morning tea at Maryanne's became a success and most weeks there were at least five women present. Maryanne told them that now that they were established, perhaps they could meet at the local cafe on High Street.

"They will give you a bottomless cup of coffee if you buy one coffee and a cake or biscuit," said Maryanne.

It became something each of them looked forward to and they were always greeted by the friendly owners, Theodora and Stavros. At midday on Wednesday as they all walked back home, Maryanne was aware that Vivienne was trying to get her alone to speak to her.

"Could you come in to my place for a moment?" she asked Maryanne. "There's something I have to tell you.

"What is it?" asked Maryanne as soon as they were inside.

"The results of the DNA test came back showing that my husband is not the father of the baby."

"What? I thought you said you hadn't had sex with any other man since before you were engaged?"

"That's right, that's what I said and that's what I know to be true. It's not something I would forget. I have never been one to have casual sex; I've had very few sexual partners."

"So what are you going to do?" Maryanne inquired.

"I'm going to ask them to repeat the test, it must be a mistake. It's probably human error."

Vivienne got up to walk to her front gate with Maryanne, and as they emerged from the front door Joanne from number 5 was parking her car in the street.

"Hello you two, how are you? I haven't seen either of you for ages," Joanne called out.

"I'm well," both the women answered in unison.

"I hear you have a regular get-together on Wednesday mornings. I'm going to get to one as soon as I can. I sometimes have days off in the middle of the week," Joanne called over her shoulder as she entered her house. "See you soon."

16

Joanne

Joanne was happy with her life as it was at present. Her position as hospital Unit Manager was demanding but she was very capable of the responsibility required. Her personal life was also to her liking as she was living with Anthony whom she was very fond of and her brother and his partner had just moved into the house. She had met Maryanne once and had taken an immediate liking to her and was interested in getting to know her more. Maryanne had revealed that she was a very experienced nurse who had held a similar position to her in a major hospital and it would be interesting for them to get together to discuss nursing.

About once a month she would roster herself on a weekend shift and have a day off during the week. That was what she was planning to do because she felt she was missing out on being friends with her neighbours. However she did invite Maryanne in to her home on a Saturday evening for a pre-dinner drink.

Joanne took Maryanne to the back garden where she had a table set with wine glasses and a plate of savoury finger food. Her boyfriend Anthony was at home and came out to meet Maryanne and poured the wine for the three of them. The late afternoon sun was still warm and shone through the trees creating a pretty moving pattern on the table cloth. Two red wattle birds chased each other in the tops of the trees then flew off, leaving the garden quiet and serene. The conversation was friendly and casual and after a few glasses of wine there was plenty of laughter. Anthony decided to make pizza for dinner and invited Maryanne to join them. The aroma of the food cooking in the kitchen was making Maryanne's mouth water.

"I didn't think I was hungry but I certainly want to eat whatever he's cooking," she said.

"Anthony is a great cook," said Joanne. "His pizzas are really different. I think you will love them."

"I love anything I don't have to cook," laughed Maryanne.

The pizzas were delicious and as they finished eating, Joanne's brother John and his girlfriend Emily arrived home. They were introduced to Maryanne and Emily quickly went off to bed leaving John watching the football on television.

Out of Anthony and John's hearing Joanne said, "I think they are having a few problems although John says they are not. Emily seems different lately, quieter than usual and sometimes withdrawn."

"Have they been living with you for long?"

"No, only about two months."

"Perhaps she would prefer them to be on their own."

"Maybe," whispered Joanne.

"Everyone seems to be having problems as far as I can see," Maryanne stated.

Maryanne went home with a full tummy that night and slept like a baby. She was woken at six o'clock in the morning by her phone ringing.

"Maryanne it's Mandy, there's trouble next door. Mildred's son and daughter are trying to get her to open the door. I know she doesn't want them there, what should I do?"

"Are they just! I'll come and speak to them," Maryanne replied.

Maryanne felt protective of Mildred now that she was aware of her terrible life and the trouble with her daughter so she did not hesitate. Pulling on her dressing gown she hurried over to stand next to Mandy in her front garden. Mildred's daughter was waiting at the front door and her son was trying the windows which were all locked.

"What are you staring at?" the daughter yelled at Maryanne.

Maryanne had thought this would happen eventually and she was prepared with what she intended to say and do. She wanted to get the situation over and done with as soon as possible.

"I am only going to tell you once, and if you don't do as I say I will ring the police."

She held her phone up to show she meant business and said, "Go away and don't come back. If I see you here again I will ring and report you. I have already spoken about you to a policewoman who is a friend of mine and I have her number on speed dial."

She stood looking at them for a few minutes then went into Mandy's home. They watched through the window as Mildred's daughter and her son drove away.

"Do you really have a policewoman friend?" Mandy asked.

"No, but they don't know that."

"Do you think they will come back?"

"Time will tell. I'll go and see how Mildred is."

Mildred had taken a sleeping pill and was not properly awake so she had not been aware of the attempted break-in. Maryanne stayed with her until she had settled back to sleep.

17

Poodles

Maryanne continued to take Mandy's baby for a walk in the evening several times a week. Sometimes Mildred went with her and sometimes Vivienne accompanied her, but mostly she was on her own. One Wednesday as she walked towards the park she noticed Jackie's two poodles chasing each other around the front garden. Jackie was not with them. As Maryanne entered the park the two dogs ran past her and began cavorting in the grass and under the old fruit trees. They ran up to the sleeping man with the dog and woke them both. The Queensland Heeler was entranced by the two other dogs and in particular the younger female, which was attempting to play with him. The other poodle ran off sniffing at something on the grass. *She might be able to smell the fox,* Maryanne thought.

Looking behind her there was no sign of Jackie so she decided when she had done two circuits of the park she would call the poodles and try to take them home. The old man stood up and called to his dog, prompting Maryanne to stop and turn around, where she saw the Queensland Heeler mating with the young female poodle.

"Come here Bobby!" called the old man. The dog ignored him and continued to do what nature intended him to do with a pretty little female on heat. They were now at the bottom to bottom stage and Maryanne and the old man stood watching. Eventually the dogs separated, sniffed at each other and began to play.

"I'll try to take them home to their owner," said Maryanne.

"Oh, they are not yours?" said the man, relief showing on his face.

"No they belong to a neighbour of mine."

Maryanne called the two poodles and fortunately they responded and followed her to Jackie's gate, which was wide open. Maryanne took them inside and rang the doorbell. No one answered so she shut the gate, making sure it was securely locked, and went on her way.

The old man began to worry that someone would not be happy to have their dog impregnated by his dog but the poodles had run up to his dog and they were obviously free, so what could he do?

18

Paternity

Vivienne rang Maryanne wanting to talk to her again about the second DNA test so they got together in Vivienne's kitchen over a cup of coffee.

"What was the result of the second test?" asked Maryanne.

"Same as the first, negative, but I'm still not convinced because I don't have any memory of having sex with anyone."

"Well, let's look at this differently," Maryanne replied.

"What do you mean?"

"Let's just assume you did have sex with someone else—who could it have been?"

"No one."

"Do you keep a diary?" asked Maryanne.

"A bit of a diary, but not with lots of detail; I use it to remember appointments, dinners out with friends, that type of thing."

"Okay, let's look at it and see what we find."

Vivienne produced her diary from last year.

"What is the date of birth of the baby? Maryanne smiled: "I was right there, but I can't remember the exact date."

Vivienne recited the date and Maryanne said, "Now we have to count back forty weeks from the birth date and see what was happening around that time."

With the aid of a calendar they counted back forty weeks and came up with a two-week period in which Vivienne could have got pregnant.

"That's interesting—that's when Marina was in hospital after giving birth to the triplets."

"Well, that's something we have worked out. Can you remember having sex then?"

"No. Phillip was away that week in Singapore for work. I've written those dates in."

"Alright, now we get down to the nitty gritty. Did anyone visit you during the time Phillip was away?"

"Yes. Tony had dinner with me a few times after visiting Marina in hospital."

"A-ha! And did you have a few drinks together?"

"Yes."

"Did you fall asleep while he was with you?"

"I'm not sure."

"Well think about it. Could he have taken advantage of you when you were intoxicated?"

"Oh come on Maryanne, I'm sure he wouldn't do that to me."

"Don't be too sure, it's happened to more women than you think."

"Besides I never drink more than two glasses of wine."

"Maybe he put something in your wine to drug you."

"I don't think so! We were all such good friends."

"So what difference does that make? Someone took advantage of you."

Vivienne's baby began to cry in the next room. Returning with the baby Vivienne sat on the couch and, putting the baby to her breast, she said, "Now that I think about it... there was one morning when I woke up in my bed partially dressed. I was wearing only a T-shirt and socks and I remember thinking that I must have had too much to drink because I would never go to bed dressed like that."

"Was that after Tony had dinner with you?"

"Yes, it was," she answered slowly. "Oh my goodness, could that be true?"

"It could be."

"I can't believe it: although he flirted with me I never gave him any encouragement at all."

"It looks like you will need to get another DNA test done with a specimen from him."

"How can I do that?"

"I don't know, but it's the only way to put an end to this and find out what happened."

Vivienne could not sleep that night worrying about what she thought could have been done to her. The more she thought about it the more she realised the likelihood that Tony had drugged and raped her. Not knowing what to do, she went over several scenarios in her mind in which she tackled Tony or spoke to Marina about her suspicions, but she did not think she had the confidence to confront either of them about such a serious matter. Also she thought it was strange that she had not had a visit from Tony and Marina since baby Maryanne had been born, considering how much she had helped Marina.

The sun was coming up and the birds were singing their morning chorus by the time she had decided what to do.

19

Joe

When Maryanne returned Mandy's baby one evening she was met by Mrs Foster waiting at her gate.

"I'm waiting for the police," she said.

"What's happened?" Maryanne asked.

"It's Joe, he won't open the bedroom door and won't answer me when I knock. I'm very worried."

"You go in and keep trying, I'll wait here for the police."

Mrs Foster went inside and Maryanne could hear her knocking and calling at the door. A police car arrived and two officers quickly entered the house. They were told of the problem and spoke kindly to Joe. When there was no response they spoke more severely and said they would have to break down the door if it was not opened soon. The door opened and Joe returned to sit on the bed. Following a long discussion with Joe and Mrs Foster, the police departed. Mrs Foster took a screw driver and removed the lock on the door, then asked Maryanne if she would like a glass of wine.

They went to the kitchen and Mrs Foster continued to cook a meal for herself and Joe.

"Would you have dinner with us?" she asked.

"Yes I'd like that," Maryanne answered. She could see that Mrs Foster wanted company and probably needed to talk. She set the table for three and called Joe, who eventually came and took a plate of food, intending to return to the bedroom.

"Don't eat in there—can't you sit with us, Joe?" Mrs Foster said kindly.

"I'll sit outside."

The two women sat inside and watched Joe through the window. A cat that had been sleeping on the table sniffed at Joe's food and began to eat off the plate. Joe stroked the cat and picked at the food but ate very little.

"I would like to tell you about Joe but I don't feel it's right to sit here looking through a window at a person and talking about that person at the same time," Mrs Foster said. "Next time Joe goes to work and I'm alone I'll come over and see you."

"What sort of work is it?"

"At a supermarket."

"I'm glad to hear that."

"Joe didn't finish school, it was during puberty that the problems began to come to a head."

"I'm interested to hear all about it."

Two days later the two women were able to get together and Mrs Foster told Maryanne about Joe.

20

Eloise

Eloise could not forget the owner of the garden centre but not wanting to rush back she took her time considering a reason to return and get his attention. Looking at the garden and all the shrubs she had planted, she knew they would look better and have more chance of thriving if they were well mulched.

At the garden centre Eloise looked about for the man in question and eventually found him sorting out fruit trees which appeared to be in need of extra watering.

"Hello," Eloise said, trying to keep her cool as she felt a rush of attraction towards him.

He looked up and smiled. "Nice to see you again. What are you after today?"

I'm after you, she thought to herself but said, "I think I need to mulch the garden."

"That's easy, come with me and I'll show you what we have."

Eloise chose the mulch, put in an order and then asked, "Would you be able to deliver the mulch because I need some advice about the garden."

"I can do that but it will have to be later this evening."

"That's perfect, thank you," Eloise replied.

Eloise knew that many men found her attractive but she was not attracted to many of them. This one was different: she was very interested in him. When she had spoken to him previously she had seen that he was intelligent, confident and funny—all characteristics she thought were important. Not to mention his good looks and lean body.

The afternoon stretched ahead and Eloise had nothing planned to make the time go by quickly. Stopping at the local shops she bought beer, wine and food to make a light meal. At home she tidied the house, watered the garden and had a shower.

I don't want to overplay this but I want him to know that I am interested in him, she thought to herself as she put on a little makeup, a pretty floral frock and sandals. Feeling nervous and excited at the thought of her expected visitor caused her to feel restless and bit silly.

Oh what the heck, she said to herself as the hot afternoon stretched on and on. Deciding that the mulch would not be delivered for ages she had time for a quick swim to cool down and fill in the time while she waited. She assumed he would deliver the mulch after the garden centre closed at six so she had plenty of time. She changed into a bikini and dived into the cool clear water of her pool.

21

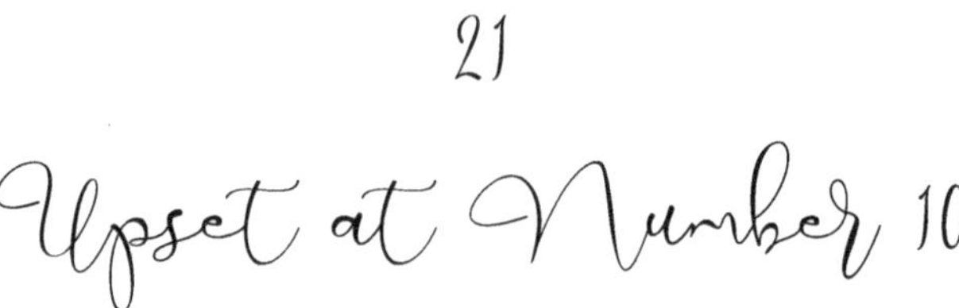

Maryanne pushed the pram carrying the baby, who was almost asleep, towards Maria's front gate. Maria handed her grandchild over the gate to her daughter-in-law and turned to smile at Maryanne.

"Everything okay with the babysitting?" asked Maryanne.

"Yes, still my husband does not know," she replied.

They chatted for a few minutes then Maryanne asked "Who lives next door to you at number 10?"

"It's a very quiet family with two school-aged children," Maria answered. "I don't see them very often, they leave early in the morning with the children in the car and are usually home late."

"I wondered if the house was empty."

"No, there is definitely a family living in there."

Maryanne entered the park and began her first circuit. The old man and the Queensland Heeler were not there today. After two circuits she walked up Apple Lane and into High Street. Sitting outside the cafe she saw the old man enjoying a pot of tea, the dog at his feet with its head resting on its front paws.

"Hello," she said to the man, who nodded and replied, "Good evening."

"Do you live nearby?" she asked.

"Yes, not far away."

"Do you mind if I join you?"

"I would be honoured," he said.

They drank their tea and chatted for about half an hour until the baby woke up and began to make little noises which Maryanne knew were going to turn into a crescendo if she didn't get moving.

"I had better get the baby back to her mother," she said to her companion. "I hope to see you again."

Walking back to Mandy's place Maryanne wondered at what the man had told her about himself. He said he had lived in the area as a child but had moved to country New South Wales as a teenager. Aged nineteen he was conscripted into the army and sent to Vietnam. He returned to New South Wales where he spent most of his life until a few months ago.

"I felt compelled to come back here," he had said.

"Have things around here changed much?" Maryanne inquired.

"Oh yes, enormously. All these shops and the new houses in High Street, they're all new to me. The houses in Orchard Lane were built when I was a child. Actually I think my father did some work for the builders."

He had not said what compelled him to return or where he was living, but he did say his dog had been with him for ten years and was his best friend.

Maryanne returned the baby to Mandy and crossed the road. As she was about to enter her front door she heard a child screaming. Stepping back to the gate she noticed a woman on the footpath wrestling with a girl of about six outside number 10. A second girl who appeared to be older was standing nearby sobbing.

"Don't go Mummy, don't go," both the children were yelling at the top of their voices.

What the woman was saying to the children was not clear. The driver's door was open and it seemed that she was trying to get into her car but the children were preventing her from doing so. Maryanne went inside saying to herself, the poor woman probably just wants a night off.

22

Eloise and Jason

Eloise went to the next Wednesday morning tea and afterwards walked home with Maryanne. When they were alone she said, "Remember the man I met at the garden centre?"

"Yes I do, have you seen him again?"

"I certainly have. Can I come in and tell you all about him?"

"Oh I love to hear a budding love story. It *is* a budding love story, isn't it?"

"I think so, and I'm so in love I have to tell someone."

"Come on then, tell me all about this new man in your life."

Eloise sat in a comfortable chair and with a smile on her face she began to tell the story.

"I went back to the garden centre and ordered some mulch and asked the owner, Jason, to deliver it. I told him I wanted some gardening advice, which wasn't really true but I thought it would make him more likely to come himself. He said he would deliver the mulch but that it wouldn't be until after six pm. Because it was a hot day and as I was expecting him to be there sometime quite late, the afternoon just dragged on and on and I was on tenterhooks. I got all dressed up and then changed my mind. I dragged my dress over my head, grabbed a bikini and jumped into the pool thinking I still had plenty of time before

he came. I was all over the place because of the excitement I was feeling.

I was floating on my back when I heard a sound at the side gate and opened my eyes. There he was standing at the side of the house. He is a most magnificent man, tall and well built, his firm body is light olive and he has dark wavy hair which was hanging over his sparkling blue eyes. All he was wearing was a very short pair of shorts and work boots. I couldn't stop staring at him and he was rooted to the spot staring at me. One of his hands was resting on the gate and the other was holding a long-handled shovel.

'Were you expecting a delivery of tan bark?' he asked with a knowing grin.

'Yes.' I replied, sliding under the water.

'Where would you like it?'

Where would I like it?

'The mulch,' he said continuing to grin.

'Over there near the gate,' I said. 'You can bring the truck down the driveway.'

He went off to move his truck and I got out of the water and put on my dress. When I opened the gate he had already backed the truck up to the gate and was leaning on the shovel waiting for me. He dumped the load then without asking he helped me to spread it. As he bent over the garden his shorts stretched over his firm bottom and his well-developed body, covered in sweat, glistened in the sun. He didn't have to help me, he just seemed happy to hang around to help and I really enjoyed watching him.

'That's about it,' he said as he turned towards me, and I noticed a soft cover of hair across his chest which descended into the top of his shorts. I was aware of something other than admiration beginning to stir inside me.

'Would you like a beer?' I asked, hoping he would stay a bit longer.

'Love one,' he replied, leaning the shovel against the veranda post.

We sat at the table on the veranda just looking and smiling at each other, not saying much, just small talk. He was very relaxed, drinking his beer slowly, and his eyes never left mine except to occasionally run quickly over my body.

'Have you recently moved in here?'

'Yes,' I said.

'Nice swimming pool,' he said and I caught sight of his pink tongue as it moved across the edge of his lips.

'Yes,' I murmured.

Suddenly he got to his feet. 'Well I have to go,' he said and he stepped off the veranda.

'Thank you for your help.' My voice sounded husky and breathless to my ears and I wondered if he had noticed.

'You're welcome, thanks for the beer.' And he was gone.

I hadn't been prepared for such a hasty departure. My senses were unsettled and my body was in the early stages of arousal. What a letdown. I must have imagined his interest in me. Well at least now I was not going to do anything I might have regretted. I picked up the two glasses from the table and turned to go inside and then I noticed the long-handled shovel still leaning against the veranda post.

After a cool shower and an hour of sleep I felt rejuvenated so I wrapped a sarong around my naked body and headed towards the fridge. I took a plate of fresh salad in one hand and a cool drink in the other and returned to the balmy night air on the veranda. Cockatoos screeched from nearby trees. A few silly moths fluttered at the light at the back door. I looked at the shovel leaning against the post and wondered what I should do with it. Should I return it? Would he send someone to collect it or would he pick it up himself? Then the front doorbell rang. I wasn't expecting visitors, I thought as I walked to the front door. Opening it I was startled to see Jason standing there. Something inside me contracted as I looked into those blue eyes which had gazed into mine that afternoon.

'I left my shovel here.'

I smiled at him. 'Come in. I was just sitting outside looking at it.'

'Sorry about that,' he added

'It's okay. Would you like a drink?'

'I'd never say no to a drink with a beautiful woman.'

'That's a line I've heard before. Will white wine do?'

'Fine.'

So there we were sitting outside on the veranda again only this time he was freshly showered, his hair still slightly damp, wearing clean jeans and a pale blue shirt and I didn't even have my knickers on.

We quickly resumed the mood of the afternoon only this time it was more exhilarating because I knew he had come back to see me and he knew he was welcome. The small talk was over between us fairly quickly because we were both focused on each other and what we both thought was about to happen. He stretched his hand over to mine and held it. Mine seemed so small in his large masculine hand. He gently pulled me to my feet. I stood over him only for a few seconds. He looked up at me and tugged at my hand again. I sat across his thighs. We kissed. His lips were delicious, just as I had imagined, and his tongue was velvet smooth. I pulled at the studs on his shirt and opened it to his waist. I can still remember the smell of his clean healthy body and the firmness of his skin. I nibbled and bit his neck and shoulders and my hands ran down his back.

He pulled at my sarong which fell to the floor. I looked down as he held my breasts one in each hand. He licked my nipples one then the other over and over again. It felt wonderful. I became drunk with desire. My hands ran over his chest down to the top of his jeans. I heard him gasp as I tugged at the stud and opened the zip. As my hand found his erect flesh I was aware of him seeking and finding the warm moistness inside me. I slowly moved onto my sarong which lay on the floor and pulled him to me.

Once he was inside me we were both lost in an exquisite passion. It was something I had never imagined I would feel. It was as if I had been waiting for this all my life. It welled up inside me until I thought I would burst. Something did burst eventually and we fell in to an exhausted sleep. Sometime early in the morning I was aware of him moving me into my bed. I grabbed at him and climbed over on to his body. That night I learnt so much about my body and desire. Up until then I had not really known much about the pleasure I could give and receive.

When I eventually got out of bed he had gone. I walked out onto the back veranda and bent to pick up my sarong. I smiled as I thought about how it got there. Then turning to go inside I began to laughed out loud as I caught sight of the long-handled shovel still leaning against the veranda post."

Maryanne looked at Eloise who gave every appearance of a woman happily and deeply in love and lust.

"Oh Eloise," said Maryanne. "You lucky woman, I'm so envious."

23

Vivienne

Vivienne thought long and hard about what she suspected had happened to her. Although at first she found it difficult to believe, after careful consideration she decided it was the most likely scenario. Tony must have drugged her and raped her when she was asleep. The more she thought about it the angrier she became. It was a violation of her body, her privacy, her friendship with Marina and her marriage. She rang Phillip and asked him to come over to speak to her as soon as he was free. Phillip was reluctant to see her but eventually he agreed.

He arrived on his way home from work, still wearing a suit. Vivienne had always liked him in a suit, wearing a collar and tie; she thought it made him look more masculine. She was disappointed when he pulled off his tie and removed his jacket. Throwing the jacket onto the couch he said, "Okay, what new story have you got for me now, immaculate conception?" He sneered as he walked across the room.

Vivienne ignored his snide remark and replied, "Phillip, when I tell you what I suspect has happened I want you to know that I'm being absolutely honest with you."

"Okay what is?" he replied cynically.

"Come and sit down." Vivienne shifted his jacket and indicated the couch beside her.

"I have been over and over this and with Maryanne's suggestion I counted back forty weeks from the baby's birth and discovered it was when you were in Singapore and Marina was in hospital with the triplets."

Phillip raised his eyebrows and looked at her, but said nothing.

"Tony had dinner with me several times after visiting Marina in hospital and it was on one of those occasions I now remember I woke the next day not able to remember going to bed. I was dressed just in a T-shirt and socks and had thought I must have had too much to drink the night before."

"So… what—you had sex with Tony and you forgot, you want me to believe that? Come on Vivienne."

"No and yes: I think he must have drugged me and raped me when I was asleep."

"Are you for real? You want me to believe that Tony would do that to you when we were such close friends?"

"I know it's awful but I think that is what must have happened. There is no other explanation. I certainly didn't have sex with anyone that I can remember."

"Jesus Vivienne, that's a big accusation you're making."

"I know. I think you should confront him and if he denies it, ask him to do a DNA test to prove that he is innocent."

"Have you got a beer?" Phillip asked abruptly. "I feel like I've been hit by a sledgehammer."

Vivienne got up and, handing the beer to Phillip, said, "So you believe me?"

He took the beer and drank most of the small bottle before saying, "I'm not sure what I believe or even what I think. I need to consider it and if I am going to ask Tony if he raped my wife, I have to be very careful about how and what I say. It's not something you ask a friend every day."

24

Jackie

Jackie called out to Maryanne as she walked towards the park pushing the pram.

"Hang on, I'll come with you ... just wait till I put the leads on the dogs."

She bent over the excited dogs and attached crimson leads to their bejewelled collars. The colour contrasted beautifully with their shiny black coats. The two women walked around the park and Jackie said, "Did you hear that commotion across the road from me the other evening?"

"Do you mean the children at number 10 screaming at their mother?"

"Yes. It was awful. I had to go over to help the father, he was almost as upset as the girls were."

"Why? What was it all about?"

"The mother, Lisa, just announced out of the blue that she was leaving them and going to live with her lover."

"Oh the poor man, and those little girls."

"Yes, they are traumatised and so is their father, Sam."

"Was he unaware his wife had a lover?"

"He told me that she recently returned to university to complete her degree and had become involved with one of the tutors. That's all he said."

"Well it happens often, so I suppose they will eventually adjust."

They walked back via Apple Lane and stopped in High Street for a cup of tea at the cafe before returning home.

25

Joanne and John

It was after midnight when Joanne's phone rang. It was her mother calling with bad news.

"Oh Joanne, it's your father—he's very sick."

"What is it Mum, what's happened to Dad?"

"He's had a heart attack and he's in hospital and is about to have surgery."

Joanne knocked on her brother's bedroom door and told him the bad news. They both got up and began searching online for bookings to fly to Adelaide as soon as possible. Arriving in Adelaide later that day they went straight to the hospital, where their mother was waiting for them.

They hugged her and asked, "How's Dad?"

"He's in the operating theatre now having stents put into his blocked arteries," she told them.

"Will he be okay?"

"Yes I think so, at least that's what the cardiac surgeon assured me, but I won't be happy until I see him awake and he's talking to me."

They were able to see him briefly in the recovery room but just for five minutes. A nurse told them to go and get something to eat and by the time they had done that he would be in Cardiac Care and they could sit with him for a while. After he woke up and they were persuaded he was okay, they went home to sleep. Both Joanne and John contacted their partners via text message telling them they would stay to keep their mother company for a few more days.

During the time Joanne and her brother were away, Maryanne saw Emily loading her car with several suitcases and a few boxes.

"Are you going away too?" asked Maryanne.

"Yes," was all Emily answered.

On the fifth day Joanne and John returned to Melbourne, arriving home at 6pm to a very quiet house. Without discussing it they had both expected their partners to be there to greet them and hopefully with a cooked meal and a bottle of wine. The house was empty and there was no aroma of an enticing meal waiting for them. After putting their bags in their rooms and looking about they realised there were a few things missing: a painting belonging to Anthony which had hung over the fireplace and several silver-framed photographs. Joanne went into the room she shared with Anthony and looked in his wardrobe and found it empty. She told John who checked Emily's cupboard and hers was also empty except for two plastic coat hangers, broken, lying on the floor.

"What on earth is going on?" John said.

Joanne looked about for a note but there wasn't one.

"It looks like they have both decided to leave us at the same time," said Joanne disbelievingly.

"That's weird. I had no idea Emily wasn't happy," said John. "What about you?"

"Maybe a little now that I think about it. He has been a bit uninterested for a few weeks or more but he said it was nothing," Joanne replied.

"Clearly it was something," John replied.

"I'm going to ring Anthony and see where he is. It's ridiculous; he could have just told me."

Joanne went into her room to make the phone call and returned ten minutes later shedding angry tears.

"John, you won't believe what has happened."

"What is it, what has happened?" he asked nervously.

"They have run off together! Anthony and Emily have run away together. He says he is sorry but they didn't know how to tell us, so when we went away they decided to go. He says they are in love and have been ever since Emily moved in."

"Jesus Christ, that's great. What a pair of cowards! They couldn't even face us."

John sat on the couch his head in his hands and began to shake. Joanne sat beside him and tried to comfort him but she was becoming more upset by the minute. Eventually they were both in tears.

"I thought we were getting married," John sobbed.

"Well it's just as well you didn't, because you would be in a bigger pickle."

26

Phillip

Phillip spoke in confidence to a friend who was a lawyer. He felt he just needed an unbiased opinion from someone to the unusual accusation Vivienne had made about Tony. His friend told him he had heard of such things happening to other women and the only way to prove paternity was a DNA test.

"He won't agree to that, he'll deny it and laugh at me," Phillip said.

"He will unless you threaten to tell his wife. If he wants to keep it from her he will probably cooperate," his friend said.

"Couldn't I just get something with his DNA on it, like a toothbrush?"

"It can be done but it's better to get him to comply. If he is innocent he will most likely agree. If he won't cooperate, then come back and see me; perhaps we will have to put some pressure on him. If he refuses to have a DNA test we will have to force him."

Phillip shoved his hands in his pockets and looked out the window. Turning to his friend he said, "I have to be very sure of what I'm going to say to him, don't I?"

"Yes you do, so I suggest that you consider what you are going to say and repeat it over and over. That way it will be in your head and you will have it like a script ready to read to him."

Phillip rang Tony that afternoon and suggested they get together for a beer the next evening after work. They met up at a pub they both knew well and sat outside in the beer garden. After exchanging the usual pleasantries between two men who had not seen each other for a while, Phillip got straight down to business.

"Last year when I was in Singapore and Marina was in hospital, did anything happen between you and Vivienne," asked Phillip.

"What do you mean 'did anything happen'? What sort of thing are you talking about?" asked Tony.

"Anything sexual?"

"Hell no; how can you ask such a thing?"

"Are you sure? Vivienne has given birth to a baby girl who looks nothing like her or more importantly nothing like me."

"I'm not the only man Vivienne knows," Tony retorted.

"Yes but she swears she hasn't had sex with anyone except me, yet there is a baby to prove she has."

"Have you had a DNA test?" asked Tony.

"Yes and I am definitely not the father."

"That doesn't mean it's me," Tony answered angrily.

"Well one other thing — the baby has olive skin and dark hair just like you."

"Has Vivienne actually accused me?"

"She is putting two and two together and it's left her wondering. She thinks she may have been drugged and raped."

Tony looked shocked. "Look, I'm getting sick of this and I'm appalled that you are even suggesting such a thing. I thought we were friends, yet here you are accusing me of having sex with your wife!" he said angrily.

"Well, someone has, and the circumstances strongly suggest it could have been you," rejoined Phillip.

Tony stood up and pointed his finger at Phillip. In a raised voice he said, "I'm going to see a solicitor and you will be hearing from him soon."

He stormed out of the garden and soon after, Phillip heard his car roar up the road. Typical Tony, arrogant and self-righteous, Phillip thought to himself as he left the pub. I didn't think he would openly admit it. If it's true, that is.

27

Lisa and Sam

Lisa and Sam had been together since meeting at university. He had studied engineering and she was had been doing an arts degree. Lisa became pregnant and ceased studying, and they decided to have another child soon after the first. Sam finished his degree and began working for a large construction company in Melbourne.

To Sam, life was perfect; he couldn't be happier, he told his friends. He loved Lisa and their two daughters so much. They moved into the house in Orchard Lane, the girls went to the local primary school and Lisa returned to university. Sam became aware of a slight change in Lisa but he did not pay much attention to it, thinking it was just the pressure of looking after the children and juggling her studies. He thought she would settle down and their lives would return to what they had been before.

The relationship that developed between Lisa and her tutor both thrilled and terrified her. It was the last thing she had expected to happen to her. It was unbelievable, amazing and totally unforeseen. Lisa was a pretty, petite, blonde woman, usually quiet and sensible. Her tutor was about ten years older than her, taller, very talkative and confident. The relationship began when Lisa asked for help with an assignment which she had found difficult to understand. Jay, the tutor, was more than happy to give Lisa some one-to-one time and so the liaison began. It became obvious to Lisa very quickly that Jay was attracted to her but never believing it would amount to anything she continued the personal tutoring.

Lisa entered the room and closed the door behind her. Jay rose to greet her as usual but instead of ushering her to a chair, Jay indicated the couch. They sat side by side and talked a little about the assignment. Suddenly Jay said "I have become very fond of you Lisa, and I wondered if you would have dinner with me one night soon?"

"Oh… maybe," Lisa blushed and then looking into Jay's eyes said, "Yes."

Jay took Lisa's hand, turned it over and kissed her open palm. Lisa looked into Jay's eyes and they kissed. So began an extremely steamy love affair between them.

Lisa could not believe the feelings that Jay aroused in her. She had always been satisfied with the lovemaking between Sam and herself but this was something else. It was like she was intoxicated or even addicted to Jay, and all her waking moments Jay was on her mind. The affair had been going on for about two months when Jay finally asked Lisa to leave her family so they could live together.

Lisa put her luggage into her car and was nervously waiting for Sam and the girls to arrive home. Her plan was to tell him and go, leaving the explanation to the girls for him to deal with, but it did not go according to plan. Sam held on to her begging her not to be hasty, to think of the girls, her reputation, her parents and anything else he could think of in his despair. The two girls got wind of the situation and began to beg their mother not to leave and all the neighbours heard; even the two poodles across the road began to bark.

28
Mrs Foster

Joe did not go to work for a few days but when he finally did, Mrs Foster went over to see Maryanne.

"Joe's story is very sad and I don't know how to help," she said.

"Before you tell me another thing, is Joe a boy or girl?" asked Maryanne.

"That's the problem. When Joe was born it was unclear if Joe was male or female. The baby had both male and female sex organs, or so it seemed."

"Ambiguous Genitalia," Maryanne said.

"Yes. There were male and female genitals present and after some tests and a lot of consultation with various medical experts and a lot of pressure from the parents, it was decided that Joe was a girl."

"At what age?"

"Wanting to get it sorted before school, about four I think."

"Was there surgery?"

"Yes, removal of the penis. I'm not sure what else—I think there is a blind vagina which remains."

Maryanne sucked in her breath. "I saw some children born with this problem when I worked at a paediatric hospital."

Mrs Foster continued, "It was when Joe was approaching puberty that the problems began. He said he had always thought he was a boy not a girl. When he confronted his parents and they told him the truth he became angry, depressed and suicidal. He kept saying he wanted his penis. He spent some time in a psychiatric institution and after discharge he refused to go home to his parents."

"Is that when you met him?"

"Yes, and I am very fond of Joe but I don't know how to help."

"I think he should go back to the hospital where he had the surgery and begin there. His medical history will still be there and he can ask for a consultation with the relevant doctors. Also if he says he is a boy, then he is a boy."

"Will they see him now that he is not a child?"

"Yes, and then they might refer him to an adult hospital and surgeon. Tell him to get a referral from his GP to the hospital general surgical department."

"Thank you Maryanne, I'll see that he does that."

I hope he can get some help, the poor boy, Maryanne thought to herself as Mrs Foster walked back across the road.

28

Joe

Joe obtained a referral and made an appointment at the hospital where he had been treated as a preschooler. Mrs Foster offered to go with him and he gladly accepted. She also suggested that Maryanne accompany them because of her background in paediatric nursing and her ability to understand the medical terminology. Joe supposed it would be of benefit to him so he agreed.

The day of the appointment came and the three of them arrived early, each anxious to get on with the discovery. They were escorted into a consultation room where two doctors were present. The older doctor began talking first, explaining that neither of them was the surgeon who had performed the operation. That man had died several years ago, one of the doctors explained.

"We have both read your medical history and have found the scenario quite surprising," said the doctor.

"Why?" asked Joe.

"Well, these days we wouldn't do that type of operation at the age you had surgery," he said. "In fact, even when you had the operation to remove your penis it was not commonly done."

"Why was it done to me then?"

The second doctor spoke: "Your medical history is very extensive and we each read it in great depth in order to make sense of what happened to you."

"What did you find out?" Joe asked nervously.

"It appears that your parents really pushed for the operation and were considering taking you to anyone, anywhere, who would do the surgery. They were members of a religious sect which influenced them. There had been prayer meetings and laying on of hands in an effort to decide your true sex. The leader of the sect made them believe this situation was the devil's work and that they could resolve the problem and eradicate the devil's power over them by removing your penis. He also said it could be a special trial from God who was testing their beliefs and commitment. He convinced your parents that by removing the penis you would automatically become a girl."

The first doctor took over and said, "It seems the surgeon did the surgery to save you from being operated on by someone inexperienced. There are signed consent forms by your parents which were witnessed by two doctors who are still working in the hospital today."

Joe had tears in his eyes as he listened to what the doctors told him. "So what happens to me now?" he sobbed.

The two doctors looked at each other and the older one said, "We have discussed that, and we have decided to offer you an EUA—an examination under anaesthetic—to see what your genitals are like now that you are an adult. Perhaps we can do something for you but we won't know until we look."

"Yes, okay—when can you do that?" asked Joe.

"My receptionist will make an appointment today and you can come in very soon as a day patient. Maybe even as soon as next week. We will fast track it because we know you are very concerned."

On the way home Joe said very little so the two women tried to keep the atmosphere light.

"Let's go to the local pub for dinner," said Maryanne.

Mrs Foster and Maryanne went to the pub and talked endlessly about Joe but he was feeling confused and miserable so he went home and sat in his room.

Joe went over the events of the day and felt annoyed and angry with his parents. In the past he had cursed them for what they had allowed the surgeon to do to him and today he had discovered it was his parents who had pushed for the operation that that had ruined his life.

"If my parents had been more like Mrs Foster this would never have happened," he said, stroking the cat which had joined him in his bedroom. The cat looked at him and purred. "You and Mrs Foster and now Maryanne are my only true friends."

30

Phillip did not hear anything from Tony so after a week he contacted him, insisting that they meet again.

"I'm not going to meet you again just to listen to your accusations," Tony replied angrily and hung up the phone.

Phillip decided to send him a text message which said, 'If you don't want Marina to hear about this I think you had better get in touch with me within 24 hrs.'

Not receiving any phone calls or messages from Tony in the next twenty-four hours, Phillip returned to his lawyer friend who promptly wrote a letter to Tony strongly advising him to comply with the request for a DNA test by the end of the month.

"Can we get the test done without his permission?" asked Phillip.

"We could get a court order, or we could be proactive and obtain a specimen without him knowing," his friend said.

"I have a feeling that's what will happen; he is never going to agree. He's too proud to admit any wrongdoing."

Phillip went to see Vivienne and told her about his interaction with Tony. "If he doesn't agree," said Phillip, "do you think you could threaten to pay a visit to see Marina and quietly pick up his toothbrush or something else?"

"Can we do that?" asked Vivienne.

"I'm not sure but it will frighten him and it should give him a bit of a shove one way or another," Phillip replied.

"All right, I'll do that because I'm determined to get to the bottom of this. I want to know who the father of my child is. And Phillip, if it is him, I don't think Marina has to know."

"Really? Don't you think she should be told?"

"Probably, yes, but then they will separate and she will be left with the three children on her own. She will suffer more than him."

"That's very kind of you to think like that Vivienne, though I certainly don't agree," Phillip said. "Anyway, you go and see Marina but let's hope we don't have to be so devious; it will be our last resort."

"I am so glad you believe me now," Vivienne answered, looking at him with tears in her eyes.

He put his arms around her and gave her a long embrace. The closeness to Philip was confusing to Vivienne; was he just comforting her as he would to anyone, or did he still love her?

31

Joe

Joe underwent his EUA a week after the consultation with the two doctors. He woke in the recovery room wondering where on earth he was. Looking around and seeing a nurse bending over a bed he remembered why he was there. He became very anxious and was keen to see a doctor with news following the EUA. Struggling to sit up he tried to get out of bed which brought the nurse rushing over to gently push him back down.

"I want to see the doctor," said Joe.

"Lie down Joe, the doctor will be in to see you soon," she answered.

"How soon?"

"As soon as he has finished the list in the operating theatre. It won't be long, they are all short procedures."

Joe settled down, keeping his eye on the door. Eventually the doctor who had performed the EUA entered and walked over. He pulled the screens around the bed and sat on a chair beside Joe.

"Joe, we had a very thorough look and I'm afraid I do not have good news for you. You do have a blind vagina but there is no penile tissue remaining." Joe stared at the doctor, saying nothing.

"The best we can do is with plastic surgery. We can fashion a penis but it will be for cosmetic purposes only, not a functioning penis," the doctor continued.

Joe lay back on the pillow staring at the ceiling.

"Do you want to go ahead with the plastic surgery?" asked the doctor.

"What's the good of a penis that just hangs there and does nothing? Who's going to see it anyway? Only me."

"Joe I want you to come and see me in two weeks' time," said the doctor gently. "By then you will have had time to consider what I've told you. If you want to go ahead with the plastic surgery, I will personally organise it for you as soon as possible in an adult hospital."

Mrs Foster took Joe home not knowing what had been discovered that day. Joe went straight to his room and went to bed. Maryanne came over to ask how the EUA had gone but was disappointed that there was nothing to hear.

"You probably should keep an eye on him. The fact that he's saying nothing could mean he has had bad news," Maryanne advised.

A day or two after the EUA Joe decided to tell Mrs Foster what the doctor had told him.

"Don't give up yet Joe, go and see the plastic surgeon and see what he can do for you."

"I don't think I will because it will just be skin, a useless dangling dick, not a real one."

"Yes but you might be happy with that; at least give it a try."

After a lot of talking Joe agreed to see the plastic surgeon, who was very sure he could make a realistic penis with the use of tissue expanders which would be inserted under the skin in the groin area to harvest skin with a blood supply. Joe went for his first treatment and had two tissue expanders inserted under the skin. He was told he would have to come back many times to have saline injected into the expanders to stretch the skin. He found it very strange and a little uncomfortable but he agreed to give it a go.

Joe began to feel a little bit optimistic and carried on with his job at the supermarket and going regularly to the hospital to have more saline injected into the expanders. One night after work he hopped off the bus and was walking home when he was confronted by the bully boys who harassed him on a regular basis. Although they had annoyed him many times before, this time he was more afraid because he could smell alcohol on their breath.

"Come on Joe, show us your pubes," one of the boys sneered at him. Joe tried to walk past but was hindered by another two boys. "What are you Joe, a boy or a girl?"

Joe dodged the second boy's arm as he grabbed at him. "Leave me alone," Joe pleaded.

"We will when we find out what's in your pants."

"No," Joe yelled as three more boys emerged from the dark and grabbed Joe, pushing him towards the fence. "Leave me alone."

The boys were determined to do what they had in mind and between them they held him, undid his jeans and pulled them down to reveal his groin area.

"Well now we know it's a girl," one of the boys yelled, jumping back to reveal Joe's nakedness to the others as they all ran off laughing.

Joe was so distressed he could hardly make his way home, and when he reached his bedroom he fell on his bed and sobbed and sobbed like a baby.

Mrs Foster heard him and rushed to his room. Sitting on the bed she tried to soothe him. He would not tell her what had happened so she lay down beside him holding him until he went to sleep.

32

Norman

Jackie waited at her gate hoping to see Maryanne with the baby. She did not have to wait long and the two of them began three rounds of the park before going up Apple Lane to High Street for a cup of tea at the cafe. The old man and his dog were seated outside enjoying a meal. He invited the two women to join him which excited the three dogs enormously.

Maryanne introduced Jackie to Norman and as she did so she remembered the day she had seen Norman's dog mating with Jackie's young female poodle Boo. Should I say something? Maryanne thought to herself. She looked at the dog in question and wondered if she was pregnant, then decided to leave it for another time.

Norman was talkative that day and told the women more about himself. He said he had left home when he was very young and one of the reasons that he had returned to the area was to see if his sister was still alive. His family had lived in the area so he thought there was a possibility she could still be somewhere nearby.

"I suppose she has married, but what is her given name?" asked Maryanne.

"I don't know if she married, but her name is Mildred," he said.

Maryanne and Jackie looked at each other and at the same time said, "Mildred?" As the two walked home together they discussed the bomb that Norman had dropped.

"I think we had better speak to Mildred before we say anything to Norman. She has had so much hardship in her life, we have to tread softly." Jackie agreed, saying, "I hardly know Mildred so I'll leave it up to you."

Maryanne returned the sleeping baby to Mandy and quickly returned to her own home to prepare her dinner. While eating a piece of salmon and salad she thought to herself: Once again I have allowed myself to become so embroiled in other people's problems; this is not how I thought my life would be back in the city. I am beginning to wonder if I have done the right thing moving back.

She poured herself a second glass of wine and put the dirty dishes in the sink. Looking out the window she saw that the garden needed watering and also noticed some weeds that seemed to have grown up overnight. I'll drink this outside with the hose in one hand and the glass in the other, she said to herself. But before going outside she was distracted by a slight stirring of a shrub in the extreme left of the garden. She continued to keep her eyes on the shrub and was surprised to see a little nose and two big brown eyes appear from beneath the foliage. Seconds later a second little face appeared, followed by the larger face of the vixen who was attempting to nudge her two cubs back into their hiding place. The cubs rolled and played together then turned to their mother to play with her. She was very tolerant and played a little but still tried to push them back into the bushes, and eventually they did as they were told.

Wow what a wonderful sight, and not one many people are privileged to observe, Maryanne thought to herself. She stood inside at the window for ages watching the family until they disappeared back into the bushes. Later Maryanne went outside to water the garden, careful not to wet the shrub where the foxes were hiding. When it was dark, she peered out of the kitchen window for ages until she was finally rewarded with the sight of the vixen emerging from the bushes and jumping over the fence.

The next morning get-together at the local cafe was very well attended. Vivienne and Mandy with their babies in prams, Maria with her grandchild, Eloise looking radiant, Jackie minus her dogs, Joanne looking very pale, Mildred and Maryanne. It was a noisy gathering and they were all enjoying each other's company so much that they decided to have an early lunch at the cafe. After everyone had had their meal Theodora came over to speak to Maria.

"Is this your grandchild, Maria?"

"Yes, my son's boy," she replied.

"*Orayo*," (beautiful) Theodora said in Greek. "I wish my children would hurry up and get married. I would love some grandchildren."

"Yes it's a blessing to see your children become parents," Maria smiled.

Theodora left Maria and returned to her work in the cafe.

Walking home Maryanne told Mildred that she had something very important to tell her. "Can I come in to your place for a chat?"

The two women sat on a seat in the garden and Maryanne reminded Mildred of the time they had walked in the park and she had been upset at the sight of the old man with his dog.

"Do you mind telling me more about why you were so spooked by the sight of that man?"

Mildred looked down at her hands clasped in her lap. She took a deep breath and said, "He looked like my husband. He had the same blue eyes and thick wavy hair just like he had."

"Okay, but it can't possibly be your husband because he is dead and would be much older than this man is anyway."

"That's true, but it gave me such a shock and reminded me of some things I would rather forget."

"Could it be someone else related to you perhaps?"

"Who?"

"What about your brother, what was his name?"

"He was called Norman."

"Well, the man from the park and I have become friends and he told me that he is looking for his long-lost sister Mildred, and his name is Norman."

"Oh my goodness — is that true, could he be my brother?"

"I definitely think he is your brother and I am hoping that you will agree to meet with him."

"I must think about what you've told me for a few days," Mildred said. "It's a lot to take in. It's not at all what I ever expected to happen."

"You let me know when you are ready to meet him," Maryanne replied. "If you are going to meet him I will tell him that I think I have found his sister. I haven't told him anything about you yet."

34

Joanne and Anthony

Joanne and Anthony had been together for four years. They had met in the hospital where she worked. Anthony was a radiographer who had worked in the same hospital but now worked for a large medical diagnostic centre. When Joanne and her brother John bought the house in Orchard Lane there had been a family renting the premises and it was not until they vacated the property six months later that Joanne and Anthony moved in. They were very happy together and sometimes talked about their future together and the possibility of them marrying and having children. John eventually moved in and after a year he brought his new girlfriend Emily to live there also.

Anthony took one look at Emily and knew he was in trouble. He had hardly glanced at another woman since he had been with Joanne but the sight of Emily's slim figure, large grey eyes and lightly freckled nose and he was smitten. He knew from the first that she had noticed him too. It was the faint blush that rose up from her neck and the way she carelessly tossed her wavy black hair behind her shoulders that told him. He could not take his eyes off her and he often found her staring at him. The two of them spent as little time as possible together but it became difficult as they were all living in the same home and sometimes, not by design, they found themselves alone in the house. It was during one of these times that the temptation became too hard to resist and they made love in a frenzy on the living room floor. Afterwards they discussed what they should do, knowing that they wanted to be together but not wanting to hurt Joanne and John. Both of them knew that no matter what or how they did it they would hurt their partners. That was why they took the easy way out and ran away when Joanne and John were absent.

Joanne was deeply upset and angry with Anthony but she seemed to be able to use the anger she felt for him to awaken dislike. She thought of all the things she did not like about him and that was what she dwelt on. He had always worn his socks to bed but kicked them off during the night, leaving them along with several other pairs until they would all appear when the sheets were changed. And that was another thing—he did very little housework and never changed the bed or washed the sheets, telling Joanne she was too fussy and she did not need to change the sheets so often. He only cleaned his teeth in the morning and he ate too much red meat and drank cheap wine. Also, after eating certain foods he got terrible wind which he thought was funny. On weekends he refused to shave and wore baggy tracksuit pants. Actually, he had stopped some of these annoying things lately and that must have been because he was trying to impress Emily, she realised.

"She can have him," she said out loud one day at work. "Beg your pardon?" said one of her colleagues who had overheard the comment.

"Nothing," she laughed. She still missed Anthony and wished he had not gone but at the same time she vowed to herself that no matter what he said or did, she would never have him back and she meant it.

John was not like his sister. He was devastated by Emily's departure, he was heart sick, unable to sleep or eat, and because of lack of sleep he was not at his best at work. He made a few small mistakes and was pulled up by the manager twice. "What's wrong John? You're not your usual self," she enquired.

"I've split up with my girlfriend and I'm not dealing with it very well," he replied. "I can't sleep."

"Do you want some time off?" she offered.

"No, it's better if I stay busy. I'll go to the doctor and get some sleeping tablets."

"Perhaps you could try something herbal first," she replied looking at him sympathetically. "I have something I can recommend."

This woman had always had her eye on John and in a way was pleased to hear he was single. Over the next few weeks she made several efforts to interest him in going out with her but he resisted all attempts so she gave up. Really he had not even noticed her overtures.

John and Emily had met at a conference where they were seated next to each other. They chatted briefly during the discussions and presentations and when they stopped for lunch they ate together. John sat opposite Emily and she smiled at him. He thought she had the appearance of something otherworldly, ethereal, someone from a fairy story. 'She should have gossamer wings,' he thought to himself as he smiled back. They kept in touch and John was determined to court her and hopefully marry her. If he made any mistake it was that he was too keen, too adoring, and frankly a pushover. Not that Emily took advantage of him, but she knew that he would bend over backwards to do anything for her. Perhaps he should not have been so obliging or so giving, maybe he should not always have let her have her own way; whatever the reason, she found him lovely but too generous and too obliging.

When Anthony and Emily realised that they had an easy way to get out of their unhappy circumstances they took advantage of the situation and quickly left. The first few days they stayed in a hotel and by the end of the week they had found an apartment on the other side of the city, away from Orchard Lane.

Both of them sent messages to the ex-partners apologising for what they had done and the way they had run off. Anthony was ready to forget Joanne and move on with Emily but Emily was racked with guilt at the way they had left. She was a sensitive soul and prided herself on being honest, kind and understanding. When she was not busy, thoughts of

John being upset with her (as she knew he would be) popped into her head and caused her to feel guilty and ashamed of herself. She tried to discuss this with Anthony but he refused to engage in the conversation, saying, "I know how you feel but we have to forget them and move on."

35

Boo

Jackie took a good look at her dog Boo and realised she had put on weight around the middle. Turning her on her back to tickle her tummy she observed that Boo's nipples had become pink and slightly enlarged.

"Oh, don't tell me you're pregnant," she said to the dog. Naturally the dog didn't say a thing, just wagged her tail vigorously.

"A visit to the vet is in order little Boo, but if you are pregnant, how on earth did you manage that?"

Later that day the vet confirmed that Boo was indeed pregnant and about halfway through, at approximately thirty days. "I don't know how this happened. She must have got out without me knowing," Jackie said to the vet.

"Well she is a very healthy dog and should do very well."

"It's not what I planned and I don't know the type of dog she mated with. I won't be able to sell the pups as poodles that's for sure," she complained.

"All puppies are beautiful and you'll still be able to sell them, just not for the same price as a poodle."

"I hope it was a Labrador; they make nice puppies with poodles."

Jackie went away feeling excited and at the same time annoyed that she had somehow let this happen to Boo.

36

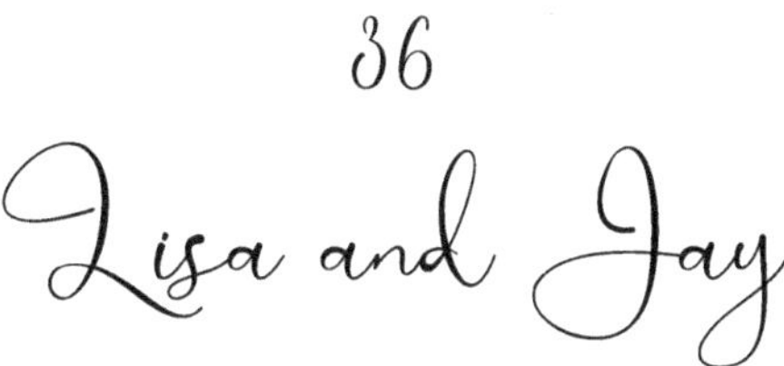

Lisa moved in with Jay and began to lavish attention on her new partner. Each day when Jay was at Uni Lisa did some of her assignments, did a little housework and then prepared an extravagant meal with wine to match. She baked cakes and biscuits and produced wonderful desserts. Jay, who was not much of a cook, enjoyed every meal that Lisa provided. After dinner they usually went to bed early and made love. Lisa continued to be besotted by Jay and although she missed her two daughters, she only went to see them once a week. Every time she went to see the girls, they begged her to stay and became extremely upset when she left. Her husband Sam could not believe that she was seeing the girls so infrequently and told her he was disgusted with her.

"They get too upset," she said.

"Of course they get upset, you've deserted them, you've broken their hearts."

Lisa told Jay that she would like the girls to live with them half the time but Jay was not keen on the idea because there was only one bedroom in her apartment.

"Well, maybe we could move into Orchard Lane and Sam could move out," suggested Lisa.

"I'm not sure he would want to do that."

"We could swap homes," Lisa added. "He could move in here. I'm going to ask him."

"That's ridiculous," said Jay. "Why would he agree to that? It's a total upheaval of his life."

"He might agree for the children's sake," Lisa asserted selfishly. Her hormones were well out of whack and she was not thinking clearly but she persisted with her idea.

37

Mildred thought about what Maryanne had told her about Norman and that he was probably her brother, and she agreed to meet him. Maryanne suggested they could have the meeting at her place so that it was on neutral ground and in private. Mildred was feeling nervous as she sat at Maryanne's kitchen table. She jumped up when the doorbell rang announcing the arrival of Norman.

"Don't get up Mildred, I'll let him in," Maryanne said, pushing Mildred gently back onto the chair.

Norman entered the room looking anxious, and his eyes quickly found Mildred sitting nervously on the edge of a chair.

"Sit down here," said Maryanne, indicating a chair at the kitchen table.

"Hello," said Norman.

"Hello," said Mildred. "Are you really my brother Norman?"

"I am, and I have no doubt now that I see you because you are very like our mother."

"Are you sure? It's a long time since you saw her."

"Yes it's a long time but I know what she looked like. When I ran away I took a photo of her with me, I still have it." He fished in his pocket and pulled out an old dog-eared photograph of a woman which he handed to Mildred.

"Yes," Mildred said, "that's her, that's our mother, oh my goodness."

They began to talk and after many anecdotes and shared memories they were sure there was no doubt, they were indeed brother and sister. By this time Maryanne had stepped outside into her garden to give them time alone. She turned on the tap and hosed the garden, making sure not to squirt the bushes where she had seen the foxes. Mildred came to the back door to thank Maryanne for finding her brother and told her she was going home to have a rest because the whole experience had exhausted her. They hugged at the front door and Norman followed Mildred through the front gate and turned right towards the park.

Later that day Maryanne received the most enormous bunch of roses she had ever seen. The accompanying card simply said, '*Thank you, you are a wonderful friend.*'

38
Maryanne

Receiving the flowers provoked Maryanne to stop and reflect on what she was doing. Really, what was she doing? Moving was supposed to have given her a new life away from other people's problems, and a chance to just enjoy a simple life. That had not happened; just the opposite again.

Why do I always become so involved in other people's problems? she asked herself, putting her nose into the centre of the bunch of flowers. As she breathed in the sweet scent, tears began to fall. Previously she had helped out several women and children who had been in need of assistance and she had suffered emotionally with the fallout. She also had some terrible memories from her time as a paediatric nurse when she had seen families fall apart when their children were very sick, or sometimes dying. She could not forget the painful treatment many children had to endure in order to be treated or cured.

Then there were the parents who took out their frustrations and anger on the nursing staff because of what was happening to their child. There had also been occasions when the parents, who were chiefly to blame for the child's injuries, were never happy no matter what she said or did. Like the boys whose parents had allowed them to play on a ride-on mower. One boy driving a mower had chased after the other who fell and was run over and lost all the skin and muscle on both shins. Or Anika, a little girl she would never forget who had been left alone in her wheelchair near a camp fire. The hand brake was not engaged and the child rolled into the hot embers. The chair overbalanced on the uneven ground and the child fell, sustaining shocking burns to both her legs. In hospital in the subsequent days, no matter what Maryanne said or did, the mother of the child criticised or complained and even yelled right into Maryanne's face. The woman's husband had sought her out and apologised for his wife's behaviour which had made Maryanne lose her composure and silent tears had cascaded down her cheeks. It was hard to take such abuse when she was very so serious about the work she did caring for sick children. Maryanne knew it was difficult for the parents who behaved the way they did; in their effort to cope, they blamed anyone but themselves. She had lost count of the times she had held back an angry retort and tears.

It was difficult to continue working and eventually she had given up a career she loved and became a practice manager in a small rural medical clinic. With the pressure and stress of the hospital behind her she threw herself into her new role. But eventually problems within the community became problems in the medical practice and often Maryanne became involved. She did not want to be involved but once she was aware of something she just could not get it out of her head until she had helped or offered a resolution. Therefore, giving the impression of being a capable aide, the other staff would seek her out for advice and guidance.

All of these experiences and incidents had left a scar on her psyche and when something happened to remind her of any of them she felt her heart sink as she fought to flick off the memory as quickly as possible.

I'm just adding to my problems here in Orchard Lane. I love the house and the people I have met here but I have to step back, otherwise I will become unwell again, she told herself.

39

Maria heard the car pull up in the driveway. She heard the door slam and the key jiggling in the front door and turning to look at her handsome husband she knew that he knew. He stood and looked at her, saying nothing. "What is it? You look upset," she said.

"I am upset. I'm upset because you have gone against my wishes. You have been taking care of the baby without me knowing. I said we would have nothing to do with that baby until Ari came to his senses."

"Oh Anesti, it's too silly, it's just a name and this baby is our grandchild. He is adorable, you would love him."

"Of course I would love him, I do love him, but that's not the issue, his name is the issue, the custom is the issue. You have done this behind my back."

"You have three other grandsons with your name and that's plenty," Maria shot back. "Your name will keep going and besides, this is an awful situation for our family to be in."

"Yes it's awful, but just a little more time and he would have changed his mind," Anesti said.

"I don't think so. Ari is just as stubborn and determined as you are. How did you find out anyway?"

"I saw Stavros from the café, he told me. Actually he just mentioned it in passing, not telling tales, he didn't know about the impasse."

"Hmm, Theodora must have said something. Well what are you going to do about it?"

"Not sure—I have to think."

Maria crossed herself and said a prayer. "I will go to the church and light a candle tomorrow, that will help."

40

Lisa and Jay arrived at number 10 each with an overnight bag in hand. Lisa knocked and let herself in with her key. Sam emerged from the back of the house and was shocked to see Lisa and a stranger standing just inside the front door. The two girls ran to their mother, throwing their arms around her waist. Lisa hugged the children to her and kissed each of them in turn.

"This is an unexpected visit," said Sam.

"I sent you an email, didn't you read it?"

"I haven't had time to open my email today, I have been too busy being a parent."

"Well can you read it now before we come in, please?"

Sam took his phone from his pocket and read the message.

Looking up he said, "Who is this?" indicating Jay.

"This is Jay."

"Jay is a woman?" he said, looking at the tall dark-haired woman who towered over both Lisa and himself.

"Yes, Jay is a woman. I thought you knew."

"And you want me to walk out and let you two move in, just like that?"

"It would be easier for the children. You can come and go as much as you like."

"This is my home."

"My home too," rejoined Lisa.

"You walked out to live with a woman and you didn't think to tell me that very important point?"

"What difference does it make what sex Jay is?"

Sam was getting very worked up, he was angry that they had just walked in unannounced, that his wife had so little regard for him that she expected him to leave his home which he had provided for her so she could live with this woman.

He was so angry he really lost his composure, saying, "Do you think I'm going to move out just so you can move in with this dyke?"

"You little weed! Don't speak about me like that," said Jay, stepping towards Sam and looming over him. "Homophobic are you?"

"Not usually," he replied.

"Sounds to me like you are, you little tiny excuse for a man."

"You can't come into my home and speak to me like that."

"I can and I will," Jay answered as she pushed Sam against the wall.

Lisa took the children into the kitchen away from the confrontation. Sam tried to evade Jay but she was stronger than him and she propelled him towards the front door, opened it and pushed him out.

Sam was beyond angry, he shook and tears welled up in his eyes. He was so humiliated, and in front of his girls and Lisa who he had loved so much. He did not know what to do. He didn't want to ring the police or even ring a friend because he was ashamed that he had been tossed out of his home by a woman. He stood looking across the road where he saw Jackie emerge from her gate and come hurrying over to him.

"What's happened now Sam; are you okay?"

"No I'm not okay, I'm really not okay." He held back a sob.

Jackie took him by the arm and guided him across the street. She steered him into her home and into the cosy kitchen where the two poodles jumped up and began wagging their tails in excitement.

"Sit down Sam, and I'll make you a hot drink."

Sam sat and noticed there were two other people in the room.

Jackie waved her hand at a man and then a young woman. "You know my husband, and this is Joanna who lives at number 5."

Sam sat and put his head in his hands. He could not stop shivering and shaking. His body was responding to the recent events in a way he had never imagined it would. Jackie handed him a cup of coffee and then offered him a glass of brandy. He downed the brandy and sipped at the coffee.

"We heard the commotion from your place because the front door was open and you were all yelling," Jackie said.

"I know we were all yelling, it was such a shock for me, I would never have believed in a million years that my wife would leave me for another woman."

"Oh, it's a woman is it?" Jackie remarked.

"Bloody women," said Jackie's husband Peter.

"Yeah, gave me the shock of my life," Sam answered, getting to his feet.

"Where are you going?" asked Peter. "You're not going over there again, are you?"

"I don't know where I'm going," he shrugged.

"Stay with us for the night," Peter offered. "We have a spare bed which you're welcome to sleep in."

Sam looked uncomfortable but he was very grateful for the offer. "That's very kind of you but we hardly know each other," he said.

"That doesn't matter. You need somewhere to sleep tonight and tomorrow you can think about what you will do."

So Sam stayed and drank a few beers with Peter and spent that night in their spare bed. In the morning he ate breakfast with his hosts and they asked him what his plans were. They also offered him the spare bed for a few more nights if he wanted it.

"I am not going to fight them," Sam said. "I'm going to move out and I'll find somewhere nearby to live so that I'm close to the girls. It's no good fighting. If that's what she wants she can have it."

"She is not the first married woman with children to have an affair with a woman," said Jackie. "I have a friend who has done much the same."

"It seems weird to me," Peter said shaking his head.

41

Vivienne

Vivienne rang her ex-neighbour Marina asking if she and Phillip could come over to see them one evening soon as they had something important to discuss with them. They agreed on a date the following week and she rang Phillip to inform him.

"Okay, let's see what happens now," he said. "He will probably be getting very nervous if he is guilty. I'll let you know if I hear from him." Sure enough, two days later Tony rang Phillip. "What are you two up to, why are you coming to see us?"

"You know why and if you don't want us to visit you and speak to Marina, all you have to do is have a paternity test."

"Jesus, mate, this is too much. Did it ever occur to you that Vivienne fancied me?"

"Yes it has occurred to me but at the moment I want to find out who the father of this child is. I don't agree with Vivienne on this but she says Marina doesn't have to know, so let's get it over and done with mate."

"Really, she said that?"

"Yeah she said that."

"How do I get a test done?"

"I'll send you the kit."

"Don't send it home, send it to my work please."

"Okay, okay just do it and let's put this to rest," Phillip replied.

Later when he told Vivienne, she told him not to be so trusting because unless one of them witnessed him putting the swab into his mouth or spitting into a container, they could not be sure it was his specimen. Phillip changed his mind and went to the office where Tony worked and handed him the kit. Tony closed the door so that his assistant could not hear their conversation and opened the container. Phillip stood directly in front of him as he read the enclosed information and carried out the instructions.

"Are you sure this isn't going to get back to Marina?" Tony asked nervously.

"That's up to Vivienne; that's what she said to me. She said she doesn't want Marina to be left alone with the triplets."

Phillip took the specimen and left the building saying to himself, he's a gutless bastard.

42

Sam

Sam went to his home the next day to gather his belongings. When he saw Lisa he said to her, "I would never have believed you would do this, you are not the woman I thought you were."

"No," she answered, "I never thought I would fall in love with a woman either."

Lisa did not want him in the house while there was no one else at home. She felt very uncomfortable and could not wait for him to leave. She didn't even ask him where he was staying or what his plans were, she just wanted him out. She had behaved shamefully and she knew it. She had not spoken to Sam before she and Jay arrived, she had lied to him, saying that Sam was okay with their moving in. Jay was annoyed that she had been lied to and told Lisa it wasn't a good way to begin their time together, and she did not want any more deceit between them.

Sam returned to Jackie's place and left his bag inside the front door. "You can stay with us until you find somewhere to live," she offered.

"Thanks, you are very kind. I'll try to get out of your hair as soon as possible, as soon as I find somewhere to live."

At Sam's workplace there were often notes on the noticeboard offering rooms to rent so he thought that would be the first place he would look.

43

Joanne

Joanne had been shocked to see Sam so upset and hear his story the night she met him at Jackie's home. They had barely spoken but she felt a great degree of sympathy for him as she had just been deserted by Anthony. She knew how he was feeling and wondered if she should invite him to her place to share a meal with her and John. They could wallow in their misery together and maybe help out by listening to him and reassuring him that he would survive.

Walking to Jackie's place the next day, she left a message for Sam inviting him to dinner the next night. She included her phone number so he could contact her if need be. Sam did ring to accept the invitation and arrived with a bunch of flowers for Joanne and a six-pack of beer for John. They had roast chicken with roast potatoes and salad all prepared by Joanne and it was delicious. After eating they sat at the table and talked for hours and were amazed at how quickly the time went and how well they liked each other. Joanne took the dirty dishes to the kitchen and called John to join her.

"We could offer him our spare bedroom. What do you think?"

John agreed and he returned to the table to ask Sam if he would like to live with them. Sam was surprised and very grateful.

"Really that's so kind of you, and it would be so convenient for me; I won't be far from my daughters and I'll feel better knowing they are just down the road if they need me."

Walking back to Jackie's house he felt humbled by the generosity of the people he had only just met in Orchard Lane and said to himself, "I haven't made any effort to make friends with any of these people and yet here they are offering help without asking questions."

44

Maryanne

Maryanne was woken by a phone call at midnight from Mildred quickly followed by a call from Mandy. Someone was banging on Mildred's window and she was sure it was her grandson. "Have you rung the police?" Maryanne yelled down the line.

"No," Mildred answered. Maryanne hung up and answered the call from Mandy.

"I've rung the police, it's time we put an end to this," Mandy said. "They will be here soon."

The police came and took the man away, promising to return the next day to interview Mildred and her neighbours. Maryanne returned to bed but could not sleep. She tossed and turned for ages and then suddenly it occurred to her that the solution was staring them in the face. Norman is the answer here, she said to herself. Why didn't I think of him ages ago.

Getting up early she crossed the street and knocked on Mildred's door, her head full of the idea that had come to her in the middle of a sleepless night. Getting straight to the point she said, "Mildred, how would you feel about having your brother live with you?" Mildred looked at her and said "I would like that very much."

"It would give you company and security and I think it's the answer to your problem with your daughter," Maryanne finished.

She only had to sew the seed of the idea and Mildred took it up and by the end of the day it was all organised. Maryanne was thankful and hoped it would take some of the pressure off her and Mandy.

Maryanne was feeling mentally weighed down and knew she needed some time out. She thought to herself, 'I'll spend a bit of quiet time alone. I am going to sit in the garden and I'm not going to answer the door or the phone for the rest of the day.'

She put a note on her front door which read "SLEEPING, NOT FEELING WELL. DO NOT KNOCK." That should do the trick she thought.

Spending more time in the garden was one of the things she always did when the weight of the world fell heavily on her shoulders, when negative feelings re-emerged and she felt her psyche was being abused. Carrying a CD player outside she played her favourite classical music just loud enough to soothe her soul while she enjoyed a pot of Earl Grey tea. The sun was shining, the air was fresh and the birds were flitting around the garden. As she sat enjoying the solitude a native thrush flew down from a nearby tree and hopped towards the deck where Maryanne was seated. It stood still for a moment with its head to one side then hopped a little bit closer to the CD player. It was listening to the music and stayed for as long as the music played. As soon as Maryanne moved to change the CD, the bird flew up into the tree and sang. What had just happened was like a burst of acknowledgement from Mother Nature and it made Maryanne's heart swell. What a wonderful way of preparing to face the day. Looking at the shrubs she wondered if the foxes were still there and if they were sleeping. She would love to see them again but had decided to let them be.

Beside her the scent from the purple blooms of a lavender bush wafted upwards and the sound of the dozens of bees busily working at collecting the nectar caused her to gaze at the industrious insects. She was reminded of a book she had loved as a child called 'Buzzy-Wings' about a bee which went out every morning to collect nectar to fill the little baskets on his back legs. She looked closely and yes, there were the little baskets she had seen so many years ago. It caused her to smile and think about her childhood and the books that had kept her company and had brought her so much pleasure. Each night she would take a pile of books to bed to read before lights out and even after her mother said her prayers with her and turned off the light, she would turn on her torch and read under the bedclothes.

Maryanne spent several days in hiding and when Wednesday came around, feeling refreshed, she emerged as if nothing had happened and went to the cafe with the other women from Orchard Lane.

Maria told her that Anesti had found out about her caring for the baby and that he was still considering what he would do about it. Eloise revealed that Jason had said he loved her and wanted to move in with her. Joanne informed them that Sam from number 10 was renting a room with her and her brother. Jackie told them that her poodle Boo was very pregnant with four puppies. Mildred announced that her brother Norman had moved in and she felt happier than she had felt in ages. Mrs Foster and Vivienne had nothing to say even though there was plenty going on in their lives.

45

Moving into number 10 was a turning point for Lisa and Jay. Instead of the relationship improving, it began to deteriorate. Jay did not like the children coming into bed to be close to their mother. She resented the time Lisa spent with them helping with their schoolwork, listening to their reading, making cakes or whatever she did with them.

"But that's what parents do," she told Jay.

"No one did that with me," Jay replied childishly.

"That's a shame," Lisa said sympathetically.

Once again Jay brought up the fact that Lisa had misled her about Sam agreeing to swap accommodation, which had led to her throwing him out. And she hated the fact that Sam was living nearby and came over frequently to see the girls. Jay really didn't like men at all, not because she was a lesbian but because as a child she had witnessed her mother being used and abused by a series of men. Her mother had always had a man in her life until she reached menopause, when she lost her desire for sex and had become a recluse in a house full of stuff. Stuff that was piled high in most of the rooms of her large house. Jay's old toys, old clothes that might come back into fashion, broken furniture, House and Garden magazines (containing ideas she wanted to use in her house) useless bric-a-brac and books, books, books. Jay stupidly blamed her mother's decline on her life with the countless horrible partners she had had. In reality, Jay's mother had been a collector of men and now stuff.

The romantic affair between Lisa and Jay was quickly losing its starry-eyed facade. Sometimes Jay did not come home and because Sam had not taken up residence in her flat, she could go there whenever she chose. Her flat was closer to the university so it was handy but sometimes she just did not want to be with Lisa the mother.

"Thank goodness Sam didn't move into my flat," she said to no one in particular as she let herself into her flat. She saw Lisa at the university and continued to be her tutor until the end of the semester and spent about four nights a week at Orchard Lane.

Lisa was perplexed by what had happened between her and Jay and soon realised that it had not been a good idea for them to move into Orchard Lane. She also knew she would not move out and desert the girls again as it had been too traumatic for them. It had been a ridiculously impulsive thing to do. She imagined that Jay would adjust to a different way of living and was not worried if she stayed at her flat in the city sometimes.

46

Having had Boo X-rayed, Jackie knew approximately when the puppies were due and began to prepare for their arrival, never letting Boo out of her sight. Early one morning Boo became quite agitated, jumping on and off the furniture. She seemed to be trying to get away from something behind her, and looking at her bottom Jackie saw what it was she was trying to escape from and put her onto the whelping box. The first puppy was born almost at once and dear little Boo took one look at the pup and began to lick it vigorously. The pup was stimulated and made a tiny noise and moved its little legs. Within half an hour Boo gave birth to another one. It took about three hours for all four puppies to appear and they all seemed to be in good health. Boo cleaned each one then settled on her side and allowed the pups to begin feeding. She just knew what to do, unlike many humans who need to be helped and sometimes do not want to breastfeed, or can't. Dogs don't mess about, they just get on with it, Jackie thought.

A day or two later Jackie called Maryanne and asked her if she would like to see the puppies, and naturally she was down there in a flash. They each had the black fur of their mother but a little grey as well.

"It's a bit too early to tell what they will look like and that might give us a clue as to who the father is," said Jackie. "At least they were not too big for her to give birth to."

"They are adorable, I would love one of them when they are ready to leave their mother," Maryanne replied, thinking once again about the day she saw Norman's dog mating with Boo and deciding once again not to say anything because it might cause trouble.

Why upset the apple cart in Orchard Lane, she laughed to herself.

47

Vivienne

Vivienne was anxiously awaiting the result of the paternity test and it was really worrying her. What if it was not Tony—who could it be? Had she done something and forgotten about it? No, that's ridiculous, she told herself. It has to be him, it fits in with the dates and her memory of waking that morning clad only in T-shirt and socks. She rang Phillip every day to see if he had received the results and he reassured her that he would contact her the minute he heard anything.

Phillip did not ring, he came to see her with the results of the paternity test in his hand.

"You should sit down, Vivienne," he said to her.

"Just tell me; stop stalling."

"The paternity test proves that Tony is the father."

Vivienne fell back onto a couch, head in hands, and began to shake. "How could he do such a thing to me and then expect to get away with it?"

Seated beside her on the couch Phillip put his arm around her. "I'm so sorry I doubted you and for the things I said to you."

"He is a pig and his selfish and disgusting behaviour has ruined our marriage and the friendship we had with him and Marina," Vivienne said between sobs.

"His behaviour is criminal and he should be put in prison for it!" Phillip ranted.

"No I want to keep it quiet," Vivienne implored. "I don't want everyone to know. What will it be like for little Mary to grow up knowing she is the result of a rape?"

At this point the baby woke and could be heard crying in the bedroom. "I'll get her," said Phillip.

The baby stopped crying as Phillip carried her into where Vivienne was seated. Phillip stood in front of Vivienne just staring into the baby's face. A broad smile broke out on her face which jolted Phillip's heart and he smiled back at her. Vivienne opened her blouse to prepare to feed Mary and Phillip put her into her arms. He sat beside Vivienne as she fed Mary and admired her confident handling and feeding of the baby. The breasts which he had loved were being used for their prime reason and as they were larger now, he found them even more beautiful.

"You are a picture of motherhood. Can I take a photo of you feeding Mary?"

"Yes if you like, but I don't want you showing it to other people."

Smiling at the photo he had just taken he said, "She is a very beautiful baby and you are a beautiful mother."

48

Phillip had gone straight to see Vivienne when he received the paternity results. He wanted to see her and make sure she had not changed her mind about telling Marina before he told Tony. He was beyond angry and disgusted with his former friend who he had thought was a better person than he actually was.

Entering the building where Tony worked, Sam's heart was beating so rapidly it felt as if it would burst out of his chest. On reaching the second-floor lobby he sat and took a few deep breaths, waiting for his heart to calm down to a level where he thought he could speak and act rationally.

Tony's assistant recognised him and indicated that he could enter the office. Tony looked up and his face paled.

"Phillip, what can I do for you?" he said as he moved towards the open door, partially shutting it. Still standing near the door he looked at Phillip sheepishly. Phillip stepped towards him and punched him angrily in the jaw. Tony fell backwards but stopped himself from falling by pushing against the door which made a noisy bang as it shut. Phillip stepped forward and hit him again.

"You gutless dog," he yelled into his face. "You drugged and raped my wife when your wife was in hospital with your triplets and yet my wife wants to keep it quiet. If you are lucky you will get away with it, so I feel justified in hitting you again." Which he did.

Leaving Tony sitting on the floor bleeding from his mouth and nose, Phillip rushed from the building heart pounding again, feeling worse, not better as he had hoped he would.

49

Vivienne

Maryanne answered a knock at the door and let in a red-eyed Vivienne carrying the baby. They sat in the lounge room together and Vivienne told Maryanne the result of the paternity test.

"I don't really know if it happened more than once because I did invite him for dinner again, and to make it worse, once Marina was home from hospital I was often in their home helping her. He behaved as if nothing had happened so how would I have ever known if I hadn't got pregnant?"

"Are you really sure about keeping it quiet?"

"Yes; I'm sure going to court and all that entails would be awful. After all, I'm all right now and I do have your namesake Maryanne," she added, kissing the baby on the top of head.

"Okay," said Maryanne, "your secret is safe with me. I won't tell a soul. There is something I meant to ask you several times but kept forgetting, were the triplets conceived naturally or are they IVF babies?"

"IVF. Marina is infertile and I know this for sure because I had to comfort her with the three IVF failures she had. She discussed all of their problems with me. She even told me she'd had unprotected sex with a number of partners and never got pregnant and was not surprised that she was infertile."

Very early the following morning there was a knock on Vivienne's front door. As she was not dressed she went to the window to see who was calling so early. Shocked, she drew back from the window and held her breath. "Marina! Oh my god what is she doing here?"

Quickly she retreated into the living room and made a phone call to Maryanne. "Can you come in please? Now? Marina is at my front door and the way she looks scares me."

"Okay I'm coming. Leave the door ajar when you let her in."

Marina looked wretched, she had the appearance of someone who had not slept for ages. She stared at Vivienne and asked, "Can I see your baby please?"

"Yes of course; come in. She's sleeping; come and see her." They headed towards the bedroom and stood over the cot. Maryanne had entered and was standing hesitantly at the bedroom door.

"Is there someone else here?" asked Marina, turning to find Maryanne behind them.

"This is Maryanne who bought your house."

Marina said nothing and turned to the cot and gazed at the baby. Tears began to fall silently down her cheeks. "Yes," she said, "she looks like my babies."

Vivienne did not know what to say so she remained silent then Marina said, "Yesterday Tony was late home and when he did arrive, he was in a bad way. His face was bruised and bleeding and he had lost two front teeth. He told me he had been attacked by a stranger in the street and wasn't intending to report the assault. I thought that wasn't like Tony but he insisted he was okay and took painkillers and went to bed. About nine o'clock I received a phone call from the wife of Tony's assistant who told me something that made me physically sick, I actually vomited. She told me her husband had heard an altercation between Tony and Phillip where Phillip accused Tony of drugging and raping you. Is this true Vivienne, did he really do that to you?"

Vivienne took Marina by the hand and led her into the living room where Maryanne was standing looking very awkward. "I'll make some coffee," she said and disappeared into the kitchen.

"Marina I wanted to keep this from you because I didn't want you to be a single mother with three small children to bring up on your own."

"How did it happen?"

"I invited Tony to have dinner with me on several occasions when you were in hospital and Phillip was in Singapore. We ate dinner and had a glass or two of wine and once I woke up the next morning in bed with just a T-shirt and socks on and no memory of the night before. I didn't put two and two together until I had given birth and Phillip refused to believe the baby was his. He had two paternity tests and they were both negative. Then I began to think about that night I just mentioned and there it was."

"But how do you know it's Tony's baby?"

"We forced him to have a paternity test and Phillip got the results yesterday. That's why he went to Tony's office. We promised Tony that we wouldn't tell you if he agreed, otherwise we were going to the police."

Marina shook her head in disbelief. "When I questioned him about it, he laughed at me and said it was all lies and you were blaming him because you had always fancied him and that you had seduced him.

"It's not a lie, it's the truth," Vivienne said. "It's awful I know, and it has ended my marriage, but at least I do have a beautiful baby."

Maryanne had made coffee and toast for the three of them so they sat at the table and quietly ate breakfast.

Marina finished eating and said to Vivienne, "I have heard what you say happened but I don't believe you; why else would you want to keep it from me? How can I not believe Tony? He is an attractive man and he says you have always had your eye on him."

"I have never fancied Tony," Vivienne shot back. "He was always a friend and no more to me, besides if I was going to have sex with him, I would have used contraception."

"Well you have a baby and you say Tony is the father and if a paternity test says that I can't disagree with science. But the usual way a woman gets pregnant is by having sex with a man. I choose to believe

Tony and I don't see how you can prove otherwise. No one saw you having sex did they?"

"Marina, I would like you to leave now. I can't convince you about how I got pregnant so there is no point talking about it any more."

Marina stood up and Vivienne continued: "So far we have kept this civil and if we keep going round and round the story we are just going to get really angry with each other, and I don't want any more anxiety or arguments with anyone."

Marina stopped at the door and said, "I'm not sure what I am going to do but I do not believe you and I would like a copy of all the paternity results please."

"I can copy them and you can take them with you today," Vivienne said and went back into the house to photocopy the papers.

Maryanne stayed for another hour and listened to Vivienne pour out her feelings of hurt and disappointment caused by people who she had loved and once felt safe with.

50
Marina

Marina sat in her car and breathed deeply, trying to regain her composure. She had been rocked by what she had found out in the past twelve hours. She had told Vivienne she didn't believe her, that she believed Tony, but deep down she had some doubts which she was fighting to keep out of her thoughts. She knew how much Tony liked sex and how frequently he wanted it and she had been away from him for weeks after the triplets were born because they had been so tiny and she was expressing her milk for them.

She had often stayed at the hospital and sometimes at a nearby hotel once the babies were well enough to be handled. She had sat beside their cribs, holding them when they were well enough and expressing milk because the sight of the tiny babies helped with the letdown reflex. I was away from him a lot, she said to herself.

51

Tony

Tony was feeling sorry for himself, what with his painful jaw and the obvious bruising all over his face. The dental bills and dental pain were pretty daunting and then there was Marina to deal with. So far, she had not said much but she had indicated that she believed him and was trying to come to terms with his being unfaithful. If only she knew that what Vivienne alleged had actually happened—he had drugged her and he'd had sex with her more than once. *God I wish I hadn't done it but it was so easy and so good.*

He remembered her beautiful body, her large breasts, dark nipples and her small triangle of pubic hair. The thought of her aroused him yet again. Jesus mate, get a grip, he told himself.

52
Emily

Emily and Anthony enjoyed the honeymoon stage of a new romance. They held hands as they walked along together, kissed frequently, and made love every chance they had. Anthony loved dining out and knew all the best fine dining restaurants in and around Melbourne. Emily was not used to such extravagance but she loved it and lapped it up. Anthony tutored her on which wines to drink with which food and what some of the obscure names on the menus were. They went to the movies, to the theatre, to pubs to listen to live bands and to the comedy festival. So much fun and so much money spent.

After a while Emily found the busy extravagant lifestyle lost its shine; coupled with Anthony's rising credit card debt they spent more time at home. Cooking together and love making were really the only things they had in common and Emily began to miss some of the things she had enjoyed with John. John was a nature lover and they had done a lot of bush walking, bird watching and nature photography together. She wondered how two men could be so different and yet she had been attracted to both of them. She realised she had not been in love with John for a long time, she just really liked him, otherwise she would not have been swept up in the escapade with Anthony.

It wasn't long before Emily found several pairs of socks in the bed linen when she changed the sheets and noticed that Anthony never shaved on the weekends. The baggy tracksuit pants she could tolerate but the excessive flatulence was too much. In her family if you passed wind you made every effort to keep it to yourself, not flaunt it as Anthony did. It was a big turnoff and because he thought it was funny she found him childish and unattractive.

"Ah come on Emily, it's just a fart. Everyone farts, even the queen," Anthony said, trying to make her laugh.

"That may be so but I'm sure she doesn't expect everyone else to be subjected to her smelly bodily functions."

Anthony had been tempted to tell her about something he had done as a teenager with his mates. After eating a meal of baked beans, they would sit on the kitchen floor holding a box of matches at the ready to light the methane as it was expelled from their bodies. Sensibly he decided it would not be a good idea to tell her.

Their love life deteriorated and their relationship became shaky.

53

Mandy was doing well as her baby was more settled and slept longer at night, making life easier for the once sleep-deprived mother. Maryanne still took the baby for a walk two nights a week but now she was usually awake and enjoyed the time gazing at the trees and listening to the birds sing as they went around the park. Maryanne stopped at the cafe on the way home for a cup of tea and sat chatting to the baby, who answered with gurgles and big smiles. As Maryanne sat, she kept an eye out for Joe coming home from his job at the supermarket but he did not appear. Returning the baby, she asked Mandy if she had seen Joe recently. She had not so Maryanne began to worry.

Knocking on Mrs Foster's door she wasn't sure what to say or ask but when Mrs Foster opened the door, she pulled it closed behind her and stood outside in the garden with Maryanne.

"Joe hasn't been out of the house for ages," she said, "not since that incident when he came home crying."

"Did he tell you what it was that upset him?"

"No, he doesn't want to talk about it at all."

"Is he going to the hospital to have the tissue expanders enlarged?"

"No, he missed the last appointment."

"What are you going to do?"

"I don't know what to do. I've had the doctor here to see him but he won't talk to her. She is organising someone from a special team that deals with psychiatric problems to come here so I'm waiting for that to happen."

"That's good, you are doing something; let's hope the appointment is soon. Please call me if you need any help at all, you know I'm always around."

She went home and poured herself a glass of wine as she prepared dinner. As she drank the wine she said to herself, you just can't keep your nose out can you? But I have to support Mrs Foster; although she is amazingly strong she is carrying that huge burden all on her own.

54

Marina's attitude towards Tony was very cool and he was well aware of the reason. She kept assuring him that everything was okay even though they both knew it wasn't. He made an effort to keep the peace and many times let things he did not agree with go by. The children kept Marina busy and because she had a nanny three hours a day and her mother was there almost every day, she was careful in the way she spoke to Tony when they were around. Tony convinced himself that with time it would all settle down and he thought he was doing a good job of placating Marina with extra attention, bottles of expensive perfume, jewellery and bunches of roses. Little did he know there was a pending eruption almost at boiling point sitting just below the surface of Marina's calm demeanour; they were both just playing happy families.

They had not made love for a while and when Tony entered their bedroom one night still holding his phone and jumped into bed fully aroused, Marina thought he could have been watching pornography. She did not say anything but the next time it happened she asked him, "What were you watching just before you came to bed?"

"I was just checking my emails," he replied.

Nothing more was said but Marina was suspicious and she knew he was up to something and that he was probably having an affair. She could not check Tony's phone because he had a lock on it and she had never wanted to access his phone before this anyway. She thought to herself that she would like to have a look but was not sure how she could.

"I've lost some photos of the babies in hospital. Can I have a look on your phone and send them to my phone please," she said holding out her hand.

"How did you lose them?"

"I deleted them by mistake. Can I have your phone?"

"No I'll send all the hospital photos to you."

"I don't want all the photos, just a few. It would be easier if I go through them."

"No I'll send them all and you can delete what you don't want."

"Okay do that then," she answered, feeling even more suspicious.

To herself she said 'I will have to be patient and vigilant to get my hands on the phone.'

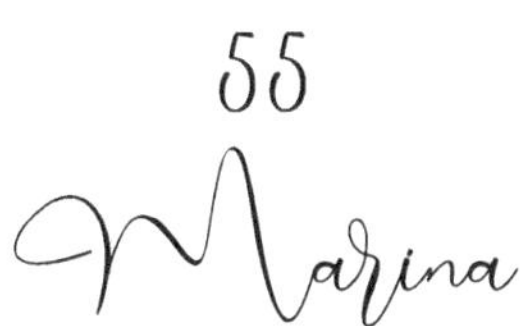

Marina went over and over the problem of how to get her hands on Tony's phone. She decided she would have to get someone else to assist her and it would have to be done in a devious way. There was no way she would ask any of her family or friends to help because she did not want any of them involved in her marital problems. The idea of hiring a private investigator did cross her mind but payment would be difficult because they presently had the added expense of the nanny. Besides, how would she explain to Tony a large amount of money being spent on their linked credit card? In the end she realised she would have to swallow her pride and ask Vivienne and Phillip for help or abandon the idea altogether. Her reasoning was that because they both despised him, they would probably be happy to help assist in his downfall.

Vivienne was surprised to receive a phone call from Marina. "Why do you want my help?" she asked suspiciously, but out of curiosity agreed to meet. After listening to what Marina had to say she was baffled.

"I'm worried that it might have something to do with him playing around and as Phillip is already on bad terms with him, I know Tony will talk to him to try to reconnect and become friends again," Marina said. "Then he will try to convince him that the sex was consensual, he is still telling me that you consented to have sex with him." Then she added "You would probably like to see him get caught, wouldn't you?"

"I will ask Phillip if he will speak to him. I won't — I don't want to speak to him ever again."

"Do you think Phillip would do it?"

"I'll talk to him but I can't speak for him. What's your plan?"

Marina had thought long and hard about how she could get Tony's unlocked phone into her hands. She explained to Vivienne that she would make sure that Tony was very drunk and almost asleep when he received a phone call from Phillip.

"He'll become very bored with the conversation and fall asleep and I will slip the phone out of his hand, take it into the bathroom, lock the door and have a good look."

"How will Phillip know when he is drunk?"

"Because I will send him a text message when the time is right."

"Sounds a bit far-fetched to me," Vivienne shrugged, "but I'll speak to Phillip and get back to you. It's a lot to ask from me after what you said the last time we saw each other, but because we were such close friends and because I dislike Tony so much I will see what we can do."

56

Phillip

Phillip laughed out loud when Vivienne informed him of Marina's request.

"What! That's a bit ridiculous. How can we do that?"

Vivienne explained Marina's devious plan. "I'm not convinced it can be done but think about it and let me know what you decide."

Phillip thought about it for a day or two then he came up with an idea of how to bore Tony to sleep. Phillip rang Vivienne: "Do you remember when Tony was studying he always insisted on reading his assignments to me asking for my input? He would read endlessly and it bored the pants off me. He really owes me for that."

She said she did remember that happening. Phillip told her that he would read a long-winded proposal he had been working on for his work. "It's very long and it's not very interesting, it would put anyone to sleep," he told her. "Even me, and I wrote it!"

57

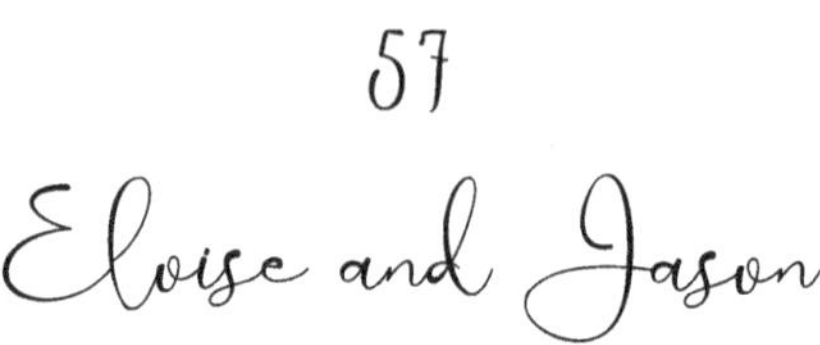

When Eloise discovered that she was pregnant both she and Jason were thrilled. As they were very much in love and had discussed marriage they decided to get married as soon as they could arrange it. The thought of a simple wedding at home in the garden and the adjoining park seemed like a no brainer. They would get permission from the local council to put up a large marquee on the park grounds next door to Eloise's house. Catering and musicians and lots of flowers could all be arranged. All the neighbours were to be invited as well as many relatives and friends of the couple.

Deciding they would need a bigger house now, Jason and Eloise hired a builder to add on a room and extend the living area of their house. They were keen to get it done before their baby was born, so before the building was started Jason cleared the garden at the side of the house which included removing a large tree. He hired a digger and on a Saturday afternoon he cut down the tree and dug out the huge tree roots. He was about to return the excess soil back into the hole he had created when he noticed a long piece of very old corrugated iron partially exposed.

'That will have to come out,' he said to himself as he reversed the digger and fronted up to dig under the iron. The iron came up revealing several planks of rotting timber which fell apart as the digger was positioned to lift it. It was at this point that Eloise came out to give Jason a cool drink. Walking towards him she stepped around the hole and glanced down.

"What's that in there?"

"Old tin and wood—must have been an old building here once upon a time."

"There is something odd in there Jason, I think you had better have a look before you dig any more."

Jason got off the digger and looked into the hole. He picked up a shovel and moved the soil around, exposing an old carpet which was rolled around something long.

"Jesus, that looks like a body: surely not!" Jason exclaimed as he pushed the carpet back exposing the skeletal remains of human legs. "Oh it is, that's awful!"

Eloise rang the police and two police officers were there that afternoon.

58

Sam

Sam settled into living at Joanne and John's house where he often had his two girls there with him. Because it was a dead-end road with virtually no traffic it was safe for the children to go back and forth between their mother and father. He and Lisa were speaking but it was very awkward; they made an effort in front of the girls.

He noticed that Jay was present less and less but was not too concerned, thinking she was busy with end-of-semester work. Lisa, however, was perplexed at Jay's absences. Jay was no longer Lisa's tutor as the subject 'Women's Studies' had finished at the end of the last semester. Lisa's questions about where she was and why she was not coming home were met with vague answers from Jay.

59

Joanne

Out of the blue Joanne received a message from Anthony stating that he was going to call in to pick up a few things which he had left at the house. She didn't think he had left anything behind but thought perhaps there was something in the garage that she had not been aware of. She was nervous about seeing him and because he had not said exactly when he intended to drop in, it put her on tenterhooks.

When he did eventually drop in it was early in the evening as Sam and his girls were having dinner with Joanne and John. It was obvious that he felt very uncomfortable when he was ushered into the kitchen and saw a man and two children sitting where he had once sat. Joanne did not care, she was glad to see him standing awkwardly in the doorway looking from her to Sam and back again.

"Well, you all look very cosy," he said self-consciously.

Joanne ignored his comment and said, "What did you leave here? I haven't noticed anything of yours."

"I left a pair of boots and a fishing rod."

"I didn't think you did any fishing," said John, looking directly at Anthony for the first time. "Must be in the garage, you know we only use it for storage."

Anthony was aware of the hostility emanating from John but asked, "Can I have the key so that I can look please?"

Joanne got up from her chair and rummaged through a drawer to find the key which she was about to hand to him but changed her mind and said, "I'll come with you."

Joanne unlocked the door and stood back to let Anthony enter. Looking around the neat interior and searching the organised shelves he did not locate his belongings.

"Why have you come?" Joanne asked. "You didn't leave one thing here and you and I both know it."

He turned to her, his face serious.

"I wanted to see you to apologise for what I did to you. I am sincerely sorry for hurting you and I am hoping that we can start seeing each other again. I miss you, Joanne."

Joanne was not so surprised by what he said, she had wondered if that was the reason he wanted to drop in and she was ready with an answer.

"What happened to the great romance between you and Emily? Did she get sick of your uncouth habits sooner than I did?"

"It didn't work out, that's all."

"I'm not sure if I'm sorry to hear that or not."

"It was a ridiculous and immature thing that I did. I know and I'm sorry."

"Yes, it was immature, and no, Anthony, we can never be together again and not even friends. What you did and the way you did it was gutless. I have moved on, as they say, and I don't miss you at all."

"Is that your new boyfriend inside?"

Joanne did not answer and was not about to explain Sam or anyone else for that matter. Walking out of the garage she locked it and returned to the house quickly, shutting the door and not allowing Anthony to re-enter.

Anthony stood looking at the closed door feeling hurt and shocked at being treated so rudely by Joanne. Turning, he acknowledged to himself that was definitely a no.

60

After dinner Maryanne often sat at the window waiting to see the fox cubs playing in the moonlight with their mother. They were quite big now but still fed occasionally from their mother who brought them dead rabbits, birds and rats to eat. Maryanne was surprised to see how quickly they were growing and how they interacted and behaved very much like dogs. They are beautiful animals, she thought, and it's so unfair the way they are treated. It's not their fault that they were brought to Australia by those silly Englishmen who wanted to hunt them. Now they have become pests and people hate them.

She remembered seeing a sickening photo in a rural newspaper of dozens of dead foxes hanging on a barbed wire fence. She had written to the newspaper protesting but had never received an acknowledgement. She knew it would be easy to make friends with the little family, all she had to do was start feeding them, but she decided that she would not.

61
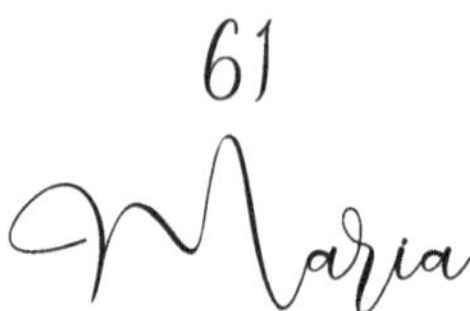

Maria and her husband Anesti talked and talked about the situation with their son and eventually Anesti realised that what Maria had been saying all along was right and that life was too short and too precious to argue with their children.

"I will fix it," he said, smiling at his wife. "I will make it okay. We will have a big celebration at Orthodox Easter and bring the whole family back together again."

Maria smiled back at Anesti. She had always known he would eventually see sense and that the family would be in harmony again.

"I am so happy, it's wonderful. We will have a lamb on the spit and all our traditional food that we love so much. I'll make the red eggs so the children can compete cracking them with each other as usual."

"Perhaps we can invite all the neighbours, what do you think?"

"Great idea! Now I'm happy and I will ring Ari at once," Maria said happily.

62
Jackie

The puppies were growing quickly and soon trying to get out of their enclosure, standing on their back legs and scratching, they whined to get out. Boo, although she was an excellent mother, often escaped from them by scaling the high sides of the enclosure and went for a wander in the garden. She had proved to be a good mother and kept her puppies plump and spotless. They all looked like they could be poodles but it was not possible to be sure what they were. Jackie still had not decided what she would do with them.

68
Plan Executed

The day Marina planned to get hold of Tony's phone was a Friday. She asked Zoe (the nanny) to come in the afternoon to keep the children occupied and not allow them to sleep. "I have something planned for tonight so I want the boys to be asleep early and stay asleep," she told her.

Zoe gave her a knowing smile thinking that Marina was planning a romantic evening with her handsome husband. "I'll do my best," she replied.

The three boys, who were just beginning to walk, exhausted themselves staggering around the furniture and attempting to walk between the couch and the coffee table. They had toddled and tottered and crawled around the garden in the sunshine and were so tired by dinner time that Marina worried they would fall asleep in their dinner bowls. Zoe ran the bath and between the two women they had the boys bathed and in bed asleep by six o'clock. Marina thanked Zoe for her help and closed the front door. Okay, she said to herself, now let's get this thing going.

During the afternoon Marina had prepared Tony's favourite meal, lasagne using his grandmother's recipe. It was in the oven and would be ready when Tony arrived home at seven. The aroma would fill the kitchen and put him in a relaxed mood. Tony loved cocktails so she made his favourite, double strength B52. A bottle of red wine was opened and standing at the ready on the kitchen bench. She knew he would be tired because Friday he always went to work early and last night he had been woken up by one of the triplets, who woke the other two, then the five of them had been up for over an hour. She had actually caused the children to wake by disturbing just one of them and felt a stab of guilt as the crying rang through the house. 'What if I'm wrong about him, what if he's not having an affair, what if this plan of mine is all for nothing?'

Tony arrived home and was thrilled to see the lasagne cooling on the table. Marina handed him a full cocktail glass and he downed it in one gulp. While he was changing, she filled the glass with another B52 and put it beside his plate. He sat at the table and Marina served them both a generous piece of the delicious pasta meal and poured them each a glass of wine. Before Tony began to eat, he drank the second cocktail. Marina lifted her wine glass towards him and made a toast to them and their beautiful boys. Tony clinked his glass with hers and downed the lot. Marina passed him the salad and poured him another glass of wine. Tony enjoyed the meal so much he had seconds and another glass of wine.

"Oh boy, I'm tired and I have had too much to drink. I think I'll have an early night," he said.

"Don't go to bed yet, I have something I want you to see," said Marina.

"What is it, can't it wait till tomorrow?"

"Last week your mother gave me a DVD of a wedding of some distant family member who lives in Western Australia. She said she wants you to look at it and give it back to her so she can pass it to your sister. Your mother will be here in the morning so please look at it."

"Oh, for god's sake, I won't know who they are. I don't know why she thinks I want to see some distant unknown relatives. Okay put it on before I fall asleep, I'm really sleepy."

Marina put on the disc and left the room. Picking up her phone she sent a message to Phillip asking him to make the phone call now. Standing away from where Tony was seated, she watched as he answered his phone and in a sleepy voice spoke to Phillip. After a few minutes his eyes began to close and he slurred, "How much longer Phil, I'm almost asleep." He continued to listen but was soon snoring with the phone still in his hand. Marina crept forward and waited; she could hear Phillip's voice droning on and Tony's snores becoming louder. As his hand began to relax the phone slipped and started to slide down his chest. Marina grabbed it and rushed to the bathroom. Making sure Phillip was still on the line she thanked him and turned on the shower to mask any noise.

First she checked his emails but found nothing untoward, they were mainly work-related. Next she looked at his messages and found nothing to worry about. His photos were mostly of her and the boys from their birth up to the present day, there were photos of past holidays and various other places they had been to but nothing she had not seen before. With a sinking feeling of guilt and annoyance she was just about to give up when she saw that he had a separate photo album, so she opened it. Her heart almost stopped beating when she viewed the first picture. It was of Vivienne—she was lying on her bed obviously asleep, a T-shirt was pulled up behind her head, her arms above her head and one leg bent up revealing her nakedness. There were several similar pictures and they did not seem to have been taken on the one day. The bed linen was different and Vivienne had on a different T-shirt, and in one of the pictures she was wearing socks. Marina quickly sent copies of the photos to her own phone then with her heart beating so fast she thought it would burst through her chest, she emerged from the bathroom and placed the phone on the floor at Tony's feet.

Marina looked at her husband slumped on the couch, his head down, chin on chest, a line of dribble leaking from his gaping mouth and she hated him. "You absolute bastard."

He mumbled something incoherent and resumed snoring.

64

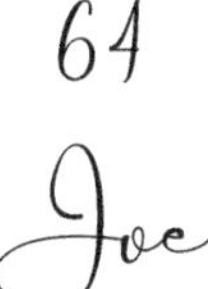

A social worker and psychologist visited Joe and spent several hours talking with him trying to persuade him to enter a psychiatric hospital for assessment and treatment. He argued that the last time he had spent time in the institution it had helped very little and had caused him to separate from his parents.

"It just brings up more unhelpful memories and thoughts. I can't see how it will help me," he argued.

"We could put a time limit on your admission," they suggested.

"How much time?" he asked.

"Two or three weeks, or a month?"

"What about one week?" he suggested. "I will consider one week only."

"That's not very long. How about we agree to one week with a review at the end of that with a possible second week?"

"Okay, but don't try and trick me. I'm not a child now."

So it was agreed that Joe would admit himself into the nominated psychiatric institution for a week with a review at the end of that week for further consultation. He packed his few precious belongings and Mrs Foster dropped him off on the following Monday morning at 9 am.

Mrs Foster notified Maryanne who suggested that because of all of the stress she had been under, they should treat themselves to a day in the city at the National Gallery followed by dinner at a good restaurant.

Mrs Foster was thrilled and so they caught a bus into the city and spent the afternoon at the Ian Potter Gallery viewing the beloved Australian Impressionist paintings which they both loved. After strolling through the shops in the city they took a tram to Carlton and had dinner at an Italian restaurant. Full of delicious food and wine they caught the bus home feeling lighthearted and happy in each other's company.

65

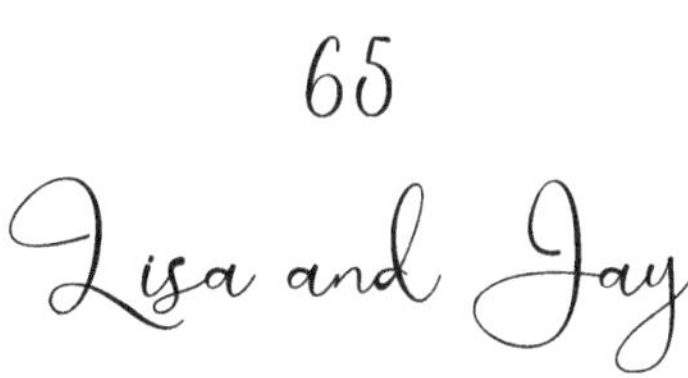

Lisa was beginning to worry about Jay's absence. She knew there was something wrong and was finding it difficult to get Jay alone to speak to her. When she was finally able to corner Jay, she was vague and unresponsive. Eventually Lisa decided to wait around until Jay had ended her tutoring session and catch her in her office. Lisa knocked on the door and tried to open it but it was locked. She must have finished early, Lisa thought to herself as she walked off to the cafeteria for a coffee. Looking up from a book she was trying to read, she was shocked to see Jay walking past the cafeteria arm in arm with a young girl who Lisa had never seen before. She jumped up and rushed outside calling to Jay, who obviously did not hear her because she put her arm around the girl's shoulders, drawing her close and kissing her on the lips. Lisa was stunned and stopped still for a moment, then gathering all her gumption she ran after the pair. When she caught up to them she said angrily, "Jay what are you doing?" The pretty young girl blushed and pulled herself away from Jay, then the three of them stood in a semi-circle and looked at each other. The embarrassed girl, realising she was involved in an awkward situation, turned and walked quickly away.

"Jay, what has happened to us?" Lisa asked tearfully

"I think it's over between us Lisa," Jay replied regretfully.

"Why? What changed?"

"I can't be with someone who has children. You are a mother and I don't fit in."

"That's silly, they are part of me and you knew I had children."

"Yes but I didn't know what it would be like having to share you with them. You give them so much of your time, time that should have been my time. They were always there in the way, asking questions, butting in, coming into our bed. Every morning I would wake up and there they were. It doesn't suit me and that's the truth of it."

"Jay, you have hurt me a great deal. I gave up so much for you and it seems it was just a game to you."

"I am sorry I have hurt you. I am fond of you but I just can't live your way of life," Jay answered as she turned to leave.

As Lisa stood and watched Jay walk away she began to shake, leading her to stumble as she made her way over to a garden seat where she sat with her head in her hands and cried bitter tears.

66

Marina did not sleep more than an hour or two the night she discovered the photos on Tony's phone. The children, who had been put to bed earlier than usual the night before, woke her very early the next morning. She struggled out of bed and began changing nappies and dressing the boys on autopilot. Sitting with them in the kitchen she fed them milk and cereal followed by a piece of orange each. She drank a second cup of coffee and thought over the events of last night. She had no idea what she was going to do. Her mother-in-law would be arriving soon as she always came on Saturday to help with the boys. By the time her mother-in-law appeared she had decided she would say nothing to Tony for the moment and this morning she would pretend she needed to do some food shopping and drop in on Vivienne.

Vivienne was surprised to see Marina so early in the morning and realised at once she must have discovered something of consequence. "What happened? Did your plan work, is he having an affair?"

"Did it ever work! And no, he's not having an affair," Marina replied as she threw herself into a chair. "You won't believe what I have found."

She began to tremble and cry. "I'm so shocked and disgusted with Tony and I hate him. I hate him so much. When I looked at him sound asleep this morning, I wanted to hit him over the head with a hammer — I didn't of course; that would make things even worse."

"Well if he's not having an affair, what has he done Marina? What have you found out?"

"Not an affair, much worse than that. I believe you now and I'm sure that he is the father of your baby—and I have pictures to prove it, and what happened to you is exactly what you suspected. I think he did drug you and rape you and worse than that, he took photos of you asleep and naked in your bed."

"Really? really? Oh my god!"

"Vivienne I'm so sorry I doubted you but now we have evidence."

Vivienne reached for her phone and rang Phillip, asking him to come over at once.

67

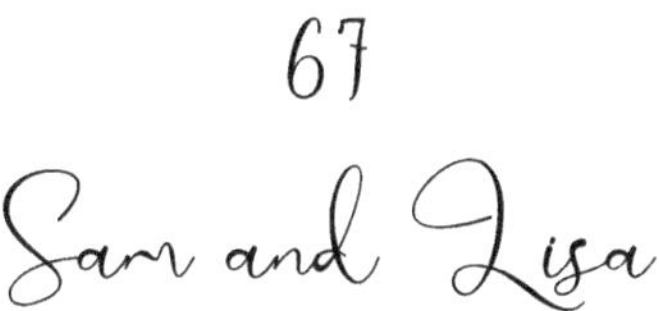

Lisa was miserable and it was not long before Sam realised she was upset. He had not seen Jay around for a few weeks so he put two and two together and asked Lisa if the relationship was over. Lisa nodded her head but could not say anything for fear of crying, and she didn't want Sam to see her in distress. He took the girls across the road to Joanne's house and left Lisa to her grief.

"Mummy's not very happy, she cries all the time," the older girl said.

"She's sad because Jay doesn't come home anymore," said the other girl. "We don't like Jay, she's too grumpy."

"Will you come back home now Daddy?"

"I don't know," said Sam. "Mummy told me to leave, remember. We will have to see what happens."

They entered the house and played a board game. They spent quite a lot of time over the road with their dad and seemed to be okay with Joanne and John who both loved having the girls in their lives.

68
Emily

Emily got in touch with John as a courtesy to inform him that she had left nursing and was about to begin studying teaching. She told him that she had been accepted at a university in New South Wales so she would probably not see him again. She apologised again for leaving him the way she had and wished him luck in his future. John replied also wishing her good fortune in her new venture and said goodbye.

69

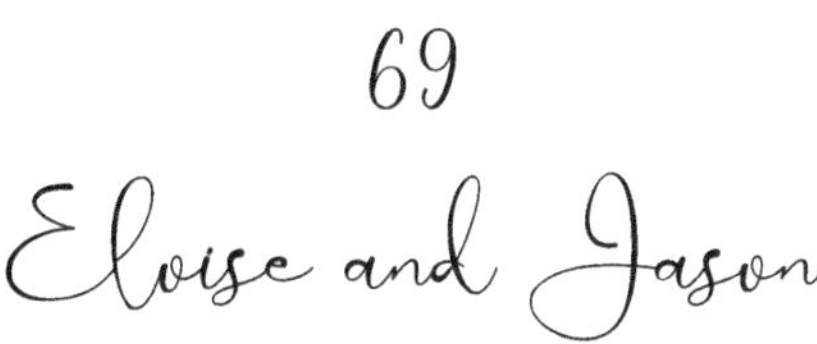

The police erected a tent in the garden around the crime scene and began to further excavate the area. The body was exhumed and because of the clothing remnants and the handbag found with the remains it appeared to be a woman. The handbag contained some documents so the police said it would not be long before they were able to identify her. There were no other bodies found in the garden and no further evidence of burials. The body was removed, the tent was dismantled, and the building work could commence.

At the next Wednesday morning tea the most popular topic of conversation was the skeletal remains and who on earth it might be. Naturally it was a shock to everyone and had quite a sobering effect on them all. When the women were walking back to Orchard Lane a tall dark man in a suit walked towards them. "Wow, who is that?" asked Joanne.

"That's James Kallas, he's the detective who has been handling the investigating Investigation," Eloise informed them.

"Hello Eloise, I have some news for you regarding the unfortunate woman you uncovered at your property."

"Do you have a name?"

"Yes, we do have a name but I can't disclose it to you until we have found any living family members. We know she lived in this area and there was a vaccination record for a baby and a bank book in her handbag so we have very good leads."

"So it won't be long before we know?"

"It won't be long; we have a name and date of birth of a baby so by the end of the day I will be looking for the relatives."

"Thanks James for letting me know. It's been on my mind constantly."

70

John

John gave up all hope of reigniting the relationship with Emily following her text message. He had not suggested it for fear of her refusal but he knew her well enough to know that she would have asked him directly if that was what she wanted.

One of the things he and Emily had once discussed was working overseas. Well I can still go, he said to himself. If she thinks it's a good idea to put distance between us I'll go one better and move to London to work.

After giving notice at his work and booking a plane fare to London, John contacted a friend he had gone to school with and surprised him with the news that he would be seeing him soon in London.

71

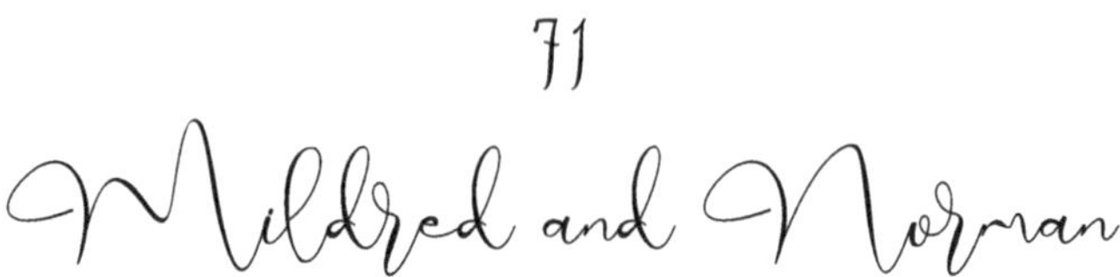

Mildred and Norman spent the morning tending a small vegetable garden they had created together. The herbs and silver beet were growing well and they picked some to cook for their dinner that night.

"I wish our tomatoes had done better, it would be nice to have a fresh tomato sandwich," Mildred said as she cut some slices of bread. "Norman, can you put on the kettle please? We can have lunch outside."

They had just sat down when the doorbell rang. "I'll get it," said Norman.

Norman returned to Mildred who was now seated in the garden pouring the tea. "Who was it?" she asked, looking up and seeing the tall dark man she had seen on Wednesday talking to Eloise in the street.

"Oh, you're the policeman, aren't you?" asked Mildred.

"Yes," he said and introduced himself. "I am Detective James Kallas. I have a few questions I need to ask you about your family."

"My family? I have no family except my brother Norman and here he is. Oh, and a daughter."

"The body that was buried has been identified and we have every reason to believe that she was related to you."

"What?" uttered Mildred. "I really don't think so. I have never had a female relative since my mother died, except for my daughter and she is still alive as far as I know."

"This woman has been buried for a long time, it couldn't be your daughter. We suspect that it's your mother."

"My mother! But she ran away with my baby sister when Norman and I were small children."

"Her disappearance was never reported to police so we have not been able to find any report of her going missing," James said.

"Why do you think it's our mother?"

"We found a bank book with her name on it and a vaccination record for a baby girl in her handbag."

"What are the names?"

"Sally Simpson and Janet Simpson."

Mildred put her hands over her mouth and exclaimed, "Oh no, Sally Simpson — that's my mother's name! I always thought she had run away. That's what our father told us, isn't it Norman." She shook her head from side to side. "Oh my god, what next? Was the baby buried with my mother too?"

"No there was no baby."

"What happened to the baby?" wailed Mildred. "That poor little baby, she had just started to walk. She was so sweet. She made us so happy the way she clapped her hands and tried to talk to us."

All this time Norman sat and said nothing. He was stunned and visibly upset by the tragic information that was being revealed to them.

James stayed and talked to Norman and Mildred for another hour and joined them for a cup of tea. He made an appointment to come back and interview them further on Monday after they had had time to digest what he had told them and to think of anything they could remember about the time of their mother's disappearance. He also requested photos of their mother and the baby if they were able to find any.

Mildred asked Norman if he would mind if Maryanne came over because she was her rock and always assisted her when she was in trouble. Maryanne as usual was only too pleased to help Mildred.

The three of them sat and talked about the shocking revelation of Sally Simpson's demise.

"Can you remember the last time you saw your mother?" inquired Maryanne.

"We saw her in the morning before we went to school, then when we returned at the end of the day she had gone and we were told by our father that she had run away," Mildred replied.

"So you assumed she had taken the baby with her?" Maryanne asked.

"Yes, naturally, and we never questioned the story," said Mildred.

"Can you remember if any of your mother's belonging or the baby's clothes and toys were gone?"

"No it was too long ago and we were both so upset. I think we were numb."

Mildred added, "If we asked any questions about our mother we got into trouble and were hit with a cane."

Norman had said very little and appeared to be deep in thought until he said quietly, "Mildred do you remember that day we saw a baby outside the bank in High Street?"

"Remind me what you are talking about."

"We were walking home from school and there was a baby strapped in a pram outside the bank. When we got close to the pram the baby smiled at us and began to clap her hands," Norman said.

"Oh yes I do remember now because we thought the baby looked like our little sister Janet, and when we walked away she began to cry," Mildred said. "We waited at the corner to see what happened and we saw the minister's wife push the pram in the other direction."

Norman continued: "We told our father and he said we were making it up and trying to cause trouble. He said all babies look alike. He was so angry with us that we were caned and sent to bed without dinner that night."

Mildred sat up straight as she said, "We never mentioned it again because we were too scared and we believed him."

"Did you ever see that baby again?" Maryanne asked.

"Yes, many times. She grew up and continued to be part of the church congregation until she left school. I think she went to university and escaped from the clutches of the church. At least that's what I was told by someone—it could have been my father. He didn't approve of girls going to university."

"Did you ever think she could be your sister after that day you saw her in the pram at the bank?"

"No, I blanked it from my mind as I was told to do," Mildred answered.

Maryanne took a deep breath and said, "I think you should ring the detective and ask him to come back to see you. It's very likely that it was your sister you saw with the minister's wife. "

72
Eloise

Eloise and Jason postponed their wedding because they felt it was not appropriate to have a wedding and celebration on the soil where a body had recently been dug up.

"We will get married after the baby is born and the renovation is completed," they decided. "It will be easier that way. The garden will be replanted and it won't be so obvious."

18

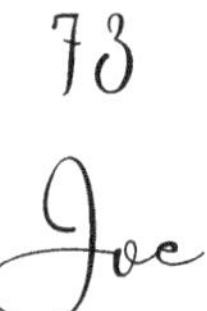

Joe

Joe spent two weeks in the psychiatric hospital and came home on different medication and seemed to be in a better mindset.

Mrs Foster was pleased to have him home and told Maryanne he was much better. When Maryanne visited him he was still quiet and spent most of his time in his room, but Mrs Foster insisted he was better because, although he had not returned to work, he was showering every day and eating his meals with her.

74
Sadness

Maryanne wheeled the pram down to the park, talking to the baby as she walked along. The baby listened and loved it when Maryanne burst into song so she sang to her quite a bit. On the second round she looked over in the distance and noticed something unusual pushed up against the fence, something golden brown that was not usually there. She pushed the pram nearer, over the grass towards the fence and had not quite reached it when she realised with a shock what it was that she was seeing.

"Oh no it's my fox, my beautiful fox!" she cried out, causing the baby to look up in alarm.

Maryanne went closer and to her horror she saw that the fox's tail had been cut off. Maryanne cried out again, "Oh no, what monster has done this to you?"

Quickly she took the baby home to Mandy and without telling anyone what she had seen in the park she went home and picked up a spade. Returning to the park and the body of the fox she began to dig a grave. Through a curtain of tears she covered the corpse and was just putting the last of the soil back over the fox when Jackie called out to her.

"Hello Maryanne, what are you up to over there?"

Maryanne turned her tear-stained face towards Jackie and replied, "I have just buried a mother fox who I have been observing for some time. Some cruel bastard killed her and chopped off her tail. Who would do that? She wasn't doing any harm."

"I think that might be my husband," she replied, "He has been trying to shoot her for ages."

"She has babies — what will happen to them?"

"He hates foxes. I don't know why but it's a thing we argue about because I love all animals."

Maryanne turned away, beginning to cry again. "I have to go home, I'm too upset," she uttered between sobs. Entering her home she thought, "What am I going to do about the fox cubs?"

75

Marina, Vivienne and Phillip

Before Phillip arrived, Marina had shown Vivienne the photos and sent them to her phone.

"I don't really want to share these pictures of you but if I don't and Tony discovers that I have them he could delete them and then we have no evidence," Marina explained to Vivienne.

"It's fine, no one will see them except the two of us and Phillip—I have to show him though," she added.

Phillip arrived promptly and when shown the photos and saw the state of both Marina and Vivienne he became really agitated. "We have to contact the police. He can't get away with this, it's criminal. He's a filthy mongrel and he can't be trusted. He could easily do it to another woman for all we know."

"Listen Phillip," said Vivienne, "I don't want this to become common knowledge and I don't think Marina does either. We have to find a way to punish him without it becoming public. If the media gets hold of this it will be all over the papers and TV and when the sensation has died down, we will be forever known as victims of Tony."

"Okay," he agreed reluctantly, "But how can we do that?"

Marina thought for a while and said "Let's meet again next week and in the meantime I will have a look at a few things. Tony has quite a few investment properties and his family have money. Leave it with me. I have to go now, my mother-in-law is on her own with the triplets."

Marina went on her way. Phillip stayed and took Vivienne in his arms to comfort her. The baby woke up and Phillip went to get her, bringing her to Vivienne who had remained sitting on the couch.

"Thank you, Phillip," she said looking up at him as he handed the baby to her.

And to the baby she said, "With all this trouble it's a wonder I haven't lost my milk supply."

16
James Kallas

Detective Inspector James Kallas took in all the new information from Mildred and Norman and felt certain they were on to something important. He was able to trace the name of the minister and his wife from the church records. After interviewing some elderly parishioners, he was told how the minister's baby had turned up quite suddenly and was said to be adopted. He was also told that the girl grew up and left the church, much to her parents' disapproval. Although her name had been changed, finding her was not difficult and he discovered she had been a teacher in the local high school until retiring just a few years ago. He went back to see Mildred and Norman again and informed them of his findings.

"I am going to contact this woman and set up a meeting with her. Her name is Carol Webster," he told them.

"Yes, Webster was the name of the minister; I had forgotten that," Mildred said thoughtfully. "Do you think she is our sister?"

"It's a possibility, and once I have spoken to her we will ask her to take a test which could prove it one way or another."

Mildred looked at Norman, who as usual had very little to say. "What do you think about that Norman, we might have finally found our baby sister. What a shame it's so late. Still I suppose it's better late than not at all."

"I'll have to speak to her first so don't get your hopes up yet. I would hate to disappoint you both," said James.

"What about our mother?" asked Mildred. "Can you find out what happened to her? I mean who killed her and why?"

"I've already spoken to the remaining elderly parishioners about that, and so far I have got nowhere. It was a long time ago so anyone who knew anything is probably dead by now. I won't give up though, I will keep trying," James reassured them, thinking to himself that it was most likely their father who had killed their mother and that it would be almost impossible to prove now.

77

Puppies

Jackie had an argument with her husband about the dead fox. He did not care what she thought and he did not care about Maryanne being so upset.

"They're vermin, pests, and they should all be killed," he argued.

Jackie gave up arguing and went off to play with Boo and her four puppies. As she looked at them tumbling and nipping and chasing each other she decided she would give one of the puppies to Maryanne. Remembering how distressed she had been in the park that day she thought, "It's the least I can do to comfort the poor woman; she is so kind and always helping other people."

Maryanne received an invitation from Jackie asking her to call in one morning to see how much the puppies had grown. Jackie put a little fluff ball into Maryanne's arms and told her to choose a puppy.

"Oh Jackie I would love one of the puppies but I will pay for it."

"No, it's a gift and I don't want any money. They will be old enough to go to their new homes in a week or two so get ready, your life is about to change." She laughed then added "for the better".

Maryanne looked at the puppies and even though they all looked alike she decided to have one of the females.

"I'll call her Vixen."

"They look like poodles but there is some other breed in there and

I will never know what it is. It doesn't matter, they are all delightful, fluffy dogs," Jackie said happily.

As Maryanne had still not told Jackie about Norman's dog mating with Boo, it was at that moment she determined she never would.

18
Fox Cubs

Maryanne contacted a Fox Rescue organisation in New South Wales to ask for advice about caring for the cubs. She was pleased to hear that she probably need not do anything because they had probably been out with their mother and most likely she would already have shown them how to hunt. "Mostly it's instinctual anyway, they get hungry and they look for something to eat," she was told.

Maryanne was pleased with what she had been advised but she was still worried about Jackie's husband and his attitude. When she went to see her puppy she confided in Jackie about the cubs.

"You said you are an animal lover and so I am hoping you will help me to catch the cubs and relocate them somewhere away from here," Maryanne said. "I think maybe near the river would be a good place to take them. What do you think?"

Jackie agreed to help her and agreed that the riverside was a good idea because there were plenty of hiding places under the bridge, in the bushes and under the fallen gums which were always left where they fell.

"I have a cage which that we can use to lure them, then we can move them easily," Jackie offered. "It would be unwise to try to catch them and handle them; they would be very scared of us and we could get injured."

So the two women lured the cubs with pieces of raw chicken and easily captured them overnight. The next morning, they covered the cage and put it into the back of Maryanne's car. On the drive to the river the cubs were quiet and still. Putting the cage down on the river bank the two women gently removed the cover and opened the cage door. Each of the cubs took a quick look at the surroundings, bounded out of the cage and disappeared into the thick tangle of undergrowth.

"That went better than I expected," said Maryanne. "I thought they might have been scared of the great outdoors."

"Remember they are wild animals after all," Jackie replied.

The two women stood and watched for a while but they never saw the cubs again.

79
Marina

Marina still had not told Tony about the photos she had found on his phone. It was really difficult to keep quiet but until she had decided what to do, she had to keep it to herself. Looking into the investment properties which Tony had acquired since they had known each other was easy because he had boasted to her about what he had and what he was worth. Marina had never been very interested in his investments, she was happy with one home to live in and a regular income. Tony had been assisted by his parents when he purchased his first two properties but subsequently he had been able to continue on his own. He had six houses in his portfolio and she looked for the most lucrative and selected two. Most of his money had been put into property investment so there wasn't a lot of money in the bank. She made up her mind about what she would do for herself and Vivienne.

A meeting was arranged with Vivienne and Phillip and she outlined what she had in mind.

"Tony has six investment properties and I am going to demand that he hands one to me and one to you, Vivienne. That will give us a substantial monthly payment from the rent or we could sell the houses and invest the money."

"He won't do that, he's too smart and too interested in money to let his investments go," Phillip observed.

"I know Tony better than you and I know his reputation is almost as important to him as his money," Marina replied. "He wants people to look up to him, he wants people to think he is a wheeler dealer who has made all the right moves without doing anything illegal. He wants to be 'the man'," Marina replied.

"Still, it's a lot you are suggesting he should give away," Phillip added.

"We still have the threat of going to the police and reporting the crime to hold over him. If we do, it will become a big story and we will all be dragged through the mud. He will lose his reputation and his money — court cases are expensive. If he doesn't do as I am asking and refuses to admit what he did, I'm sorry Vivienne but I am going to make sure it becomes a media sensation. I've decided I will not allow him to get off scot free. Imagine how he will feel if his family find out what he did to you. His mother and grandmother who adore him will be horrified and I know he would do anything to keep them happy."

"I think we should get some legal advice so we have it documented, and remember, we always have the DNA tests and the photographs," Phillip said. "I will go back to see the lawyer who advised us before and see what we can do."

The lawyer said that what they were proposing was a bit unorthodox but he would draft a letter to Tony and have it hand delivered. When he did not receive a response from Tony, he notified Phillip and said he had made an appointment to see Tony the following Wednesday, and that Tony had also engaged a lawyer so the meeting would be held between the two legal men.

80
Sam and Lisa

Lisa became depressed and was unable to function normally. She found it difficult to get out of bed and most days dragged herself around the house in her pyjamas and dressing gown. She did not eat and did not shower and was neglecting the girls. Sam knew he had to step in and take over so he moved back into their house. He realised very quickly that Lisa was in an extremely bad way and persuaded her to see her GP. Lisa agreed to take anti-depressants if Sam would agree to stay with her. He did so, and he even took two weeks of annual leave to care for her.

Lisa slowly began to improve and the children were happy to have both parents at home again. If they were aware of the seriousness of the situation they didn't let on, even though Sam was not sleeping in bed with Lisa. The girls snuggled up with her and kept her company when they came home from school. Lisa loved her daughters and looked at them and wondered what on earth she had been thinking when she left them for Jay. She smothered them in kisses and cuddles.

When Sam and Lisa were alone one day, she looked at him and said, "Sam, I am so grateful to you for what you have done for me. I know I don't deserve it but I am really so appreciative. I don't know what got into me with Jay—it was almost like I was under a spell. I changed and it was like I was intoxicated and mad all at the same time. I didn't see things rationally; I was harebrained and stupid and—" Lisa began to cry again.

Sam looked at her, his Lisa who he had loved and adored and trusted with his life, and he knew that what she was saying was the truth, and he felt only love and sympathy for her. He put his arms around her and held her until she stopped crying.

"Let's just take it easy for the time being and we will sort it out," he murmured. To himself he thought, maybe we can put it behind us and go back to happier days.

81
Maria and Anesti

It was time to celebrate the Orthodox Easter and as Maria and Anesti had decided, it was to be a very big party. Their son Ari was quietly pleased to hear that his father had changed his attitude about the baby's name. He had always known his father to be a sensible man and knew he would eventually see that there were plenty of little Anestis running around in their family.

All the women in the family got together and worked out what food they would contribute to the day. They wanted to have dancing so a friend of the family was asked to bring his band to play Greek music.

Anesti got up very early on Sunday morning to put a lamb on the spit so it would be cooked for lunch time then he made tzatziki, which is delicious with lamb. He had hung the yogurt the night before to remove the whey and now he grated cucumber, squeezed out the excess water, chopped herbs and garlic and added olive oil until it was just right.

The previous day Maria had prepared Easter bread, tsourekia, and baklava as well as three dozen dyed red eggs. Getting up early with Anesti she peeled and chopped two trays of potatoes to roast. The daughters-in-law made huge bowls of salad and shortbreads called kourabiethes which were laden with slivered almonds and drenched in icing sugar.

The day was fine and all the visitors arrived by midday. The children were kissed and fussed over by the adoring adults then off they ran to play and explore in the park. Two of the older aunties sat on folding chairs at the gateway to the park, talking and laughing loudly as they kept an eye on the excited children. There were so many people the house was full of noise and laughter. All the residents of Orchard Lane were there with the exception of Joe. "I just couldn't persuade him," Mrs Foster said sadly. Mandy's girls and Sam and Lisa's girls knew each other from school and played happily with the other children.

After lunch was over the music began and most of the women got up and danced. As the afternoon went by the men danced on their own, spinning and hitting the floor. One old man danced with a beer bottle balanced on his head amusing everyone, specially the children who laughed and pointed in amazement. The children were told not to try the bottle on the head trick as it was too dangerous. Everyone laughed as one little Anesti found a bottle of water which he attempted but failed to balance on his head.

Maryanne, Vivienne, Joanne and Mandy did their best to learn the steps of the Greek dances. They got the hang of one dance and the music changed and so did the steps. Joanne was determined to master the steps so remained in line with the other people. Someone moved in beside her and took her hand but as she was busy observing the other dancers, she did not see who it was until the music stopped. Looking to her left she found herself looking into the eyes of James Kallas. They had not been introduced but each of them had noticed the other in Orchard Lane when James had come to speak to Eloise.

"Oh, I didn't expect to see you here," said Joanne feeling pleased and happy to be holding his hand.

"I went to school with Maria and Anesti's son Ari," he said dropping her hand.

"Are you here on your own?" she asked, looking about hoping there wasn't a woman accompanying him.

"Yes, on my own, just finished work. I got someone to take over from me."

They stayed together and chatted then when the music changed, they danced a slow dance together.

"Well look at that," said Eloise.

"What, where?" asked Maryanne, as then she spotted Joanne and James dancing together almost cheek to cheek. "Ah, that's nice."

Jackie announced that she had given a puppy to Maryanne and asked Lisa and Sam if they would like one of the puppies for their girls. Lisa hugged Jackie, thanking her profusely.

"They will be so thrilled," she said calling the two girls to her side and telling them that Jackie had something to ask them. When they heard what she had to say to them they both jumped up and down and squealed with delight.

"Really? We can have a puppy? When can we have it?"

"'Tomorrow," said Jackie, "Come over after you've had breakfast and choose one. Maryanne has already chosen one but there are still three to pick from." The girls ran off to tell the other children.

"I'm not sure who to give the other two puppies to. What do you think?" she asked Maryanne.

"Mandy's girls would probably like one and maybe Joe would benefit from a pet to care for," Maryanne suggested.

"Yes that's a good idea. Let's ask Mrs Foster." Looking around, she was nowhere to be seen. "She must have gone home early," said Maryanne.

It was getting late and people with children were beginning to leave. Joanne seemed reluctant to go home and why should she? James steered her to a quiet part of the garden and they sat together and talked and smiled at each other.

"I'm very tired, so I'm going home now," announced Maryanne.

"We will walk with you," said Norman, looking around for Mildred.

They said goodnight and headed up the lane towards home. As they approached their end of the lane an ambulance turned and stopped outside Mrs Foster's house. The lights were on but the sirens were not operating so whatever was the matter it must not be an emergency, Maryanne thought. Two ambulance officers exited the car and went quickly to the front door of Mrs Foster's house.

Maryanne, Norman and Mildred stood still in the middle of the road and watched anxiously. "Is it Joe or Mrs Foster who is not well?" Norman said.

A few minutes passed then Mrs Foster came to the door, her eyes red from crying and her face streaked with tears. She held out her arms to Maryanne and sobbed. "It's Joe: he's dead."

82

Marina

Once Tony was aware of the request being put to him, he became quite edgy. He arrived home early and asked Marina, "What have you been up to? What's all this I hear about two of my houses being given away? Do you think I'm mad? I haven't worked and saved hard to give them away to you or Vivienne. It's ridiculous, the stupidest thing I've ever heard!"

"When you get the whole story you will change your mind, I hope. Otherwise we are all going to be besmirched because of what you did to Vivienne."

"Come on Marina, I told you it was consensual sex—she was willing."

"No Tony, she was not willing. I believe you drugged and raped her and now there is proof."

"What proof?" he demanded.

"Photographs."

"What photographs?"

"Photographs of Vivienne unconscious on her bed."

"So? Anyone could have taken photos like that."

"They were on your phone Tony."

Tony looked startled. He lifted his hand and, pushing the hair back from his forehead, he said, "No one has access to my phone so they can't be my photos."

Raising her eyebrows knowingly Marina retorted, "There are ways and means."

"Jesus Marina, what have you done?"

"What have *you* done Tony. You have ruined our marriage and if this gets out and becomes common knowledge you will have ruined your reputation and made all of us, including your family, a laughing stock in the community. Plus, as you know, you should go to jail for what you did."

Tony was red with rage. He opened the fridge and removed a bottle of wine and took it with him into his study. He was too drunk to eat dinner that night and he slept in his chair in the study. During the night he fell to the floor where he found himself in the morning. Groaning, he struggled to his feet and dragged himself to the bathroom. Looking in the mirror he saw the bags under his eyes, his unshaven face and dishevelled hair and said to his image, 'You bloody idiot, you bloody idiot.'

In the morning he contacted his lawyer who told him that he was getting off lightly considering he had committed such a serious crime.

"You will end up in jail if you don't go along with what they are asking," the lawyer said. "The cost of a court case will break you so I'm advising you to take the deal. You are lucky you have an escape route."

83

Carol Webster

James Kallas met Carol Webster and put forward the information he had regarding Mildred and Norman. He explained the situation and was surprised at her answer.

"I wouldn't be at all surprised at what my parents had done; they were both strange and my mother never questioned what my father did or said," Carol told him. "My father was dishonest and had no respect for other people, particularly women, and he pushed and cajoled people to get what he wanted."

"Would you be willing to have a DNA test to see if you are related to Norman and Mildred?"

"Yes, certainly I will," she replied.

James received the results and straight away he visited Mildred and Norman to tell them they had a sister living not far away who was very keen to meet them. All three were eager to get together as soon as possible and chose the cafe around the corner in High Street as a first meeting place. Mildred and Norman arrived early and asked Theodora to prepare an afternoon tea that was fit for such an auspicious occasion. When Carol Webster entered the cafe both the women had tears in their eyes and the three of them hugged in a circle. Theodora brought a large teapot to the table and poured tea for them then left them alone. As they tucked into the afternoon tea of ribbon sandwiches and little cakes, they asked questions of each other and filled in some of the gaps of their lives. Mildred remembered Carol as a child but sadly Carol could not remember Mildred even though she had been involved in the Sunday school. They told her about the day as children that they had seen her outside the bank and how they had been forced to forget her. Carol revealed she had never been told she was adopted and when Mildred informed her that they had been told their mother had abandoned them, her eyes filled with tears again as she said, "Our poor unfortunate mother, I wonder what happened to her?"

"There is no doubt that she was killed and probably by our father," Norman answered sadly. "What a tragedy. I do have a photo of her, would you like to see it?" he said removing the dog-eared picture from his pocket.

Carole blinked back tears as she viewed the photo of a mother she had never known about until recently. "I wish I could have known her," she said quietly.

Finishing their afternoon tea, the three siblings walked around to Mildred's house. Carol was invited in and as there was still so much to talk about, she stayed for dinner and did not leave until quite late.

84

Tony

Tony tried to fight the demands which were being made of him but once he was shown the photographs he began to back down. Marina threatened to show the pictures and the DNA results to his parents and, because he did not want them to know, he began trying to negotiate a better deal for himself. Again his lawyer advised him that he was getting off lightly and would most likely end up in jail if Vivienne reported his crime to the police.

"Marina, I will agree to give one property to Vivienne but not to you — we are still together, aren't we?"

"Do you really think I can stay with you after what you did?"

"Marina please, try to forgive me. I know what I did was wrong but you were in the hospital all the time and I was lonely."

"That's pathetic! And no excuse for committing a criminal act like that; it's awful. Aren't you ashamed for taking advantage of Vivienne? She is a good person and she was a good friend to both of us."

"Yes I am ashamed, very ashamed, and very sorry."

"Do you realise that it's because she cares about me and my situation that she didn't go to the police?"

"I know. She really is a good person, even better than I thought."

"Aren't you only sorry because you have been caught?"

"No Marina, I am truly sorry and very ashamed. If I was a good Catholic I would probably go to confession."

"Why don't you go to confession?"

"Because I don't believe in confession, you know that. I am telling you, though, that I'm sorry and I will do anything to convince you to believe me and forgive me and stay with me."

"I don't know, Tony, I just don't know. I feel as if you are asking far too much of me. I have to decide what is best for me and the three boys. That's the bottom line—me and the boys."

85
Maryanne's Son Steven

Maryanne's son had kept in touch with her following the letter revealing he was returning to Australia. Maryanne had not thought too much about it because she had been so busy with the comings and goings of Orchard Lane. She knew he was coming and she was looking forward to seeing him and his wife Hilary, little Benji and the new baby. Steven said he would spend a week with his mother before travelling to Kelvington to begin work. He had already organised a house to rent and he intended to buy a new car in the city before moving north to his new life.

They arrived in the evening and were exhausted from the long flight from the UK. Hilary said it had been very uncomfortable sitting in a plane for fifteen hours caring for a baby and a small child and Maryanne did not doubt it. She had prepared beds for them in her spare room and Steven, Hilary and the baby went to bed as soon as they had eaten, but Benji was not sleepy and stayed up with Maryanne playing with fluffy little Vixen.

86

Funeral

The funeral for Joe was hardly a celebration of his life because his life had been cut short by misfortune, mismanagement and mistakes.

It was held in a local non-denominational chapel which had floor-to-ceiling windows framed by trees and shrubs. The sunlight filtered through leaves that moved slowly as the wind gently shifted the branches to and fro. The atmosphere was sombre as people gathered in small quiet groups. The voice of Eva Cassidy singing Somewhere Over The Rainbow played softly in the background as an usher encouraged people to be seated. Maryanne and Mandy sat on either side of Mrs Foster and the other residents of Orchard Lane were seated behind them. On the other side of the aisle were people unknown to the residents and most assumed rightly that they were related to Joe. A couple in their forties sat huddled in the front seat and Mrs Foster told her friends that they were Joe's parents. A celebrant began the service and covered Joe's life with delicacy and respect, then asked for anyone who would like to say anything about Joe.

Mrs Foster stood and went forward, holding a handwritten note. Taking a moment to compose herself, she began to speak.

"I have known Joe since he was fourteen years old. He came to live with me after treatment in a psychiatric hospital when he felt he was unable to continue to live at home. He was a lovely, gentle boy who loved animals and birds and never did a bad thing while he was with me. We kept each other company, played board games and watched movies together, but he was never really happy. He was one of those people who has had been let down by many people just because he was different. He didn't fit into a mould — you could say he was a square peg trying to fit into a round hole. This is a reminder, or a lesson, for all of us to be tolerant and understanding of people who are different and let them be who they are. If we have not experienced something, how do we know how it feels? If someone is not like the majority, does that really matter? And who are we to judge anyway? Most people in Orchard Lane were kind to Joe and I am very grateful for their support, in particular Maryanne and Mandy who helped me many times. If we expect to be treated with respect and tolerance, we must give respect and tolerance. I loved Joe like he was my own son and I will miss him every day. Thank you," she said, dabbing at her eyes.

Sitting down, Mrs Foster put her hands over her face until she regained her composure, Maryanne and Mandy on either side of her.

An informal gathering held at the cafe in High Street was very generously given by Steve and Theodora. The food was plentiful and tasty and the wine flowed freely, enabling people to relax and open up with each other. The subject of Joe's death and how he died was uppermost in the conversation of some individuals, whereas others preferred not to dwell on his suicide. Mrs Foster did not want the way he died to become common knowledge — she said it was enough to know that he was feeling so wretched that he ended his own life. Joe's parents were in agreement. Not even Maryanne knew how he died.

Jackie arrived with one of her puppies and asked Mrs Foster if she would like the puppy which she had intended to give to Joe. Mrs Foster put out her hands and taking the puppy in her arms, she hugged and kissed the fluffy little animal.

"You couldn't give me a better gift," she said. "I would love to have the puppy and he or she shall be called 'Joey.'"

Jackie handed her a bag containing food for the puppy and some dog toys. When Mildred was preparing to leave, she was approached by Joe's mother who said she remembered her from the church they had both attended. She said she remembered Mildred helping out with the young children when she was one of the youngsters herself. Mildred did not remember her because she had forced herself to forget most of those people and the memories associated with that part of her life.

The residents of Orchard Lane walked home in small groups, deep in thought, reflecting on what little they known about Joe and wondering if they could have done more to help him. If only, if only…

87

Change of Heart

Maryanne entered the sanctity of her home, and throwing herself into a comfortable chair she stuck her legs out in front of her and threw her arms down at her sides. Trying to relax she took deep slow breaths in and out, in and out, but she could not relax. Her puppy Vixen was put into her lap by Benji who also managed to climb into the space. The puppy climbed up to Maryanne's face and licked it all over which made her laugh. She allowed the child to get comfortable and the puppy snuggled in between the two of them. There was a story book nearby which she picked up and began to read to Benji. LITTLE BROWN GIRL GOES FOR A WALK. It was a story about a little red hen who walks around the farmyard meeting other animals. Benji tried to guess what sounds the animals made as he snuggled close into Maryanne's side, where his warm body helped her to relax. She fell asleep with the little boy in her arms.

The next day Steven decided to drive to Kelvington to view the house he had rented and pay a visit to the medical centre in which he would be working. Maryanne said she would like to accompany him so with Benji for company they set out on the hour-long trip north to the Macedon Ranges. Maryanne had not been there since moving to Orchard Lane. As she looked around at the green hills and heard noisy birds in the tall gums in the forest, she began to wonder how she had left such a beautiful place.

Steven stopped at the real estate agents' office to pick up the key and sign some papers relating to the rental agreement. The office was busy so while they waited Maryanne looked at the houses that were listed for sale in the area. There were the usual properties for a regional area: big houses on large allotments, small farms, villas and empty blocks. Many of them looked similar although they were different types of properties and nothing stood out at all except one. A miner's cottage on the outskirts of Kelvington was offered for sale at a price she could afford. She knew this cottage and had always admired it as it was being restored and renovated by a young couple from Melbourne.

"I didn't expect to see that house for sale," Maryanne said to the agent, Josie.

"Unfortunately the couple have separated and have to sell, it just came on to our books yesterday morning."

"I know the house; when I lived here I always admired it as I drove past on the way to the village shops."

"Would you like to view it?" Josie asked.

Maryanne thought for a second before replying, "Yes I would."

Steven went to the medical centre and Maryanne and Benji went to see the miner's cottage with Josie.

The cottage had a white picket fence and a cottage garden filled with roses, lavender and perennials. A climbing rose grew up one of the posts of the veranda which stretched across the front of the house shading the front rooms as well as a casual table and chairs placed on the deck. There was a central front door leading into a hallway with two rooms opening on either side and ending in a large open living area with high ceilings. Glass doors leading out to the garden let in light, and the kitchen to one side was well equipped with new appliances and plenty of storage and bench space. A deck at the back extended from one corner of the house to the other and was roofed with beams and see-through material creating a pleasant shaded outdoor area. Beyond was a small garden planted with native plants, a few fruit trees, herb patch and a chicken coop.

"This is perfect. I'll buy it."

"Really? I didn't think you were looking for a house," said the astonished agent.

"I wasn't, but I just decided I want to move back to the area and this house is perfect for me," Maryanne replied as she watched Benji run around in the pretty garden. Maryanne could hear frogs, so walking around outside she peered over the fence where there was a large fish pond situated in the garden of an old house in the distance. 'That's a sound I have missed,' she said to herself. Returning to the little cottage she inspected the three bedrooms and bathroom, finding everything was in excellent condition and she would not have to change a thing. She felt a pang of regret for the couple who had done all the work and now had to abandon it; once again she was going to enjoy a home where a couple had intended to make their lives. All their hard work, a newly renovated house, a well-planned garden, and she had not had to do any of the hard labour—she wouldn't even have to paint a wall. Feeling excited she returned to the office with Josie and proceeded to set in motion the purchase of the cottage. Steven picked her up from the office and they went to a nearby cafe for a late lunch. When Steven heard about the purchase he was flabbergasted.

"I thought you had decided to stay in Orchard Lane?"

"Yes I had, but I have changed my mind. I'm moving back to the area I love. I probably shouldn't have moved away in the first place."

As they ate their lunch a flock of cockatoos screeched and played in the nearby gum trees. Some of the birds hung upside down flapping their big white wings which revealed the delicate yellow feathers beneath. Benji, having never seen such birds, was entranced by their clown-like antics.

"If you like these birds, you will love the kangaroos. I know where we can probably see some: would you like that?"

"Yes!" Benji yelled, "I want to see kangaroos!" He jumped off his chair and began to hop around.

Maryanne directed Steven to an area where they could walk in the bush and in a very short time they found kangaroos, an echidna and a blue-tongued lizard. Benji, tired from all the fun and activity, fell asleep on the way home. This gave Maryanne and Steven a chance to talk about all that had happened in Orchard Lane since she had moved in.

"I can see why you want to go back to semi-rural living," Steven said.

Maryanne did not tell any of her friends in Orchard Lane of her decision to sell and move back until the day before a For Sale sign was due to be displayed on her property. It was a Wednesday at the weekly morning tea that she announced her intention to move. Everyone was shocked and disappointed at her decision. She did not tell them that first the death of the fox and then the added trauma of Joe's death was the tipping point, or that she was finding it difficult to cope with the burden of their dependence on her. Instead she said it was because Steven and Hilary needed her back in Kelvington. Mildred and Vivienne nearly cried and begged her to change her mind and Mandy said she would miss her help in the evenings but she understood that family should come first. Mrs Foster said she was considering moving herself and not to be surprised if she ended up in Kelvington also. "I would love to see you there," said Maryanne, who worried more about Mrs Foster than any of the others.

Maryanne was so glad to get inside and be on her own with her family. Although she loved her friends in Orchard Lane they were sapping her energy.

88
House for Sale

The house was viewed by several young families and one or two middle-aged couples but the person who bought it was an elderly retired teacher called Carol Webster. Maryanne was pleased Carol had bought the house, knowing it would be good company for Mildred and Norman. After all, they had missed out on a lifetime of being together. Now they would be able to see each other every day if they wanted to.

The residents of Orchard Lane got together to plan a secret party to farewell Maryanne. Most of the residents wanted to have the party at their own respective homes so to solve the problem they put names in a hat and pulled out Joanne.

89

Farewell

Although people were looking forward to the party it meant they were one day closer to Maryanne leaving and no-one was looking forward to that. Mandy crossed the road to speak to Joanne and offered to contribute to the party food. They settled on quiche and salad, then Mandy mentioned how much Maryanne had helped her and that she would miss her assistance.

Joanne replied, "Sometimes there is a person in your life who you rely on or lean on and when this person is no longer present it seems like a gaping hole has opened up. Eventually that gap will be filled in because some of us will develop strategies to fill the deficit. This is something I have experienced many times in my workplace. A nurse who you like to see on the same shift as you because she is experienced, conscientious and helpful is someone you hate to see leave, but eventually you manage without them."

"Yes I know I will cope, but I will never forget what she has done for me and my children."

The day of the surprise party came around and Maryanne was invited to Joanne's for a pre-dinner drink. She arrived at five o'clock and was pleased to see Vivienne there and even more surprised to see more of the residents arriving over the next half hour, until they were all there. It was crowded and noisy and lots of fun. Maryanne gave each of the friends her new address and told each of them they were welcome to visit her once she was settled in.

James Kallas, who now lived with Joanne, cooked on the barbecue and poured drinks. Sam and Lisa, who were still working out their relationship, were there with their two little girls. Lisa, who had lost weight when she first split up with Jay, was looking better. Vivienne said she and Phillip had discussed getting back together and that he was so taken with baby Maryanne that he had been visiting them almost every night of the week and bringing gifts for her and the baby.

"What has happened between Marina and Tony?" asked Maryanne.

"She made him move out and they are having counselling but it's not easy for her," Vivienne said. "She still doesn't know if she can forgive him but she says she will try for the sake of the three little boys."

"If she is able to forgive him and they get back together she is a better woman than I am," Maryanne answered sharply.

Jackie brought the last of the puppies and offered it to Mandy who had been hoping she would get one of the fluffy little bundles. Her daughters were beside themselves with joy and ran around in circles chanting "Puppy, puppy, puppy."

Maria and Anesti were thrilled to see James and Joanne together because he had been friends with their son Ari since the boys were twelve years old and was like one of the family to them. Eloise, now heavily pregnant, sat in a comfortable chair, feet up on a stool, hands caressing her abdomen and with Jason hovering nearby bringing her drinks and tidbits to eat.

Mildred and Norman brought their sister Carol with them and she seemed to fit in beautifully with the other residents of Orchard Lane. Theadora and Stavros arrived late after closing the cafe and brought some delicious food with them. Mrs Foster, who had not looked well since Joe's death, was quiet and just sat and listened to the conversation, not joining in at all. Everyone except Mrs Foster had gone home by ten o'clock; she stayed back to offer a helping hand to Maryanne with packing her china and glassware in the following week.

"We can have a long chat as we work," she suggested as they left Joanne's front door.

90

Two days later Mrs Foster crossed the road with her puppy and spent the morning helping Maryanne wrap all her breakables and pack them into boxes ready for the move. She was talkative and Maryanne realised she had probably wanted this time with her to get a few things off her chest. They had lunch together watching the two puppies play together before beginning on the linen cupboard and Maryanne's wardrobe. Sitting at the table Maryanne told her about the foxes she had had in the garden and confided that when she found the dead vixen this was when she had first thought of selling and moving away from Orchard Lane.

"It was the death of Joe that really pushed me," she said. "One death was bad enough but two, and I just felt like I had to get away."

This prompted Mrs Foster to talk about Joe's suicide and how he had died. She had not intended to tell but she felt as if Maryanne deserved to know as she had been so supportive and caring to her and Joe. Not thinking how the whole truth might further upset Maryanne, she launched into the awful details of his demise.

"He really wanted to die, he was determined to end his life," she said. "He had just had enough of unhappiness and lack of tolerance. Many people were kind to him but the fact that so many others were not, affected him badly. Apparently he was subjected to bullying by at least one person at work. He felt that he didn't fit in anywhere and thought he never would. The bad experiences of the past and recently ate away at his resilience until he just couldn't face any more ridicule and lack of understanding. It was, as they say, soul destroying."

Maryanne listened and then asked, "Did he write these things in a letter before he died?"

"No, but he did tell me and the psychologist that was how he felt. I was worried and so was the psychologist, she spoke to him almost every day over the phone. He was adamant that he wouldn't go back to the psych hospital. It's because I was worried about him that I didn't stay very long at Anesti and Maria's party. I feel so guilty because if I hadn't left him he would still be alive."

Maryanne looked at Mrs Foster and said, "I think all the things that happened to him from way back until now caused him to develop paranoia and he imagined every sidewards glance or any little offhand remark was aimed at him personally. He could have done it another day when he was alone. You can't blame yourself. It was bound to happen at some stage. He was a tortured soul; it's just so sad."

In a high-pitched, wailing voice Mrs Foster cried, "Oh Maryanne, he hung himself, and when I walked into the kitchen I could see through the window his body hanging from the beams on the veranda. I rushed outside and tried to lift him but it was too late, he was well and truly dead. It was awful, absolutely awful, and it's a sight I will never be able to erase from my mind. Every time I look outside at the place where he died I'm filled with guilt and misery. I don't think I can stay in that house; I will have to sell, I don't know where I will go though. I might end up in Kelvington one day."

Maryanne took her in her arms. They clung together both weeping for Joe and the sadness of his life; the mistakes that were made and the damage that had been done to him through misunderstanding and ignorance.

Maryanne broke away from Mrs Foster and went to the kitchen to boil the kettle and make a pot of tea. "Let's sit outside in the garden and enjoy the fresh air," she suggested. "I always find solace in the garden with the birds and the wind in the trees. It helps me to calm down."

Sitting together they did not speak until Maryanne said, "Take some deep breaths, in and out … in and out… now listen: can you hear the sound of the bees buzzing in the lavender?"

They were both silent again until a native thrush began its melodious song from a tree next door. Once again it was like a gift from Mother Nature attempting to lift their spirits, and it did—a little. Maryanne pointed out the bush where the vixen had lived with her cubs. Quietly she said, "I miss seeing them in the garden at night."

The two friends returned to packing for a few more hours but neither of them mentioned Joe again.

91

Leaving

A large removalist van arrived early on a Monday morning and quickly packed all of Maryanne's boxes and furniture inside the cavernous vehicle. When the men had finished and Maryanne had completed a last-minute clean, it was time to go. Most of the neighbours were outside to wave goodbye to Maryanne, who they kissed and hugged, promising to keep in touch or visit soon. Maryanne put the puppy Vixen into a harness in the back seat and drove behind the van as it turned left into High Street.

As she began her journey back to the Macedon Ranges, she looked in the rear vision mirror and noticed a smaller van enter Orchard Lane. It stopped outside Mrs Foster's house. A man in overalls got out and began putting up a For Sale sign on her fence.